Violet
and the
SMUGGLERS

Harriet Whitehorn

Illustrated by Becka Moor

THIS BOOK BELONGS TO

....

SIMON AND SCHUSTER

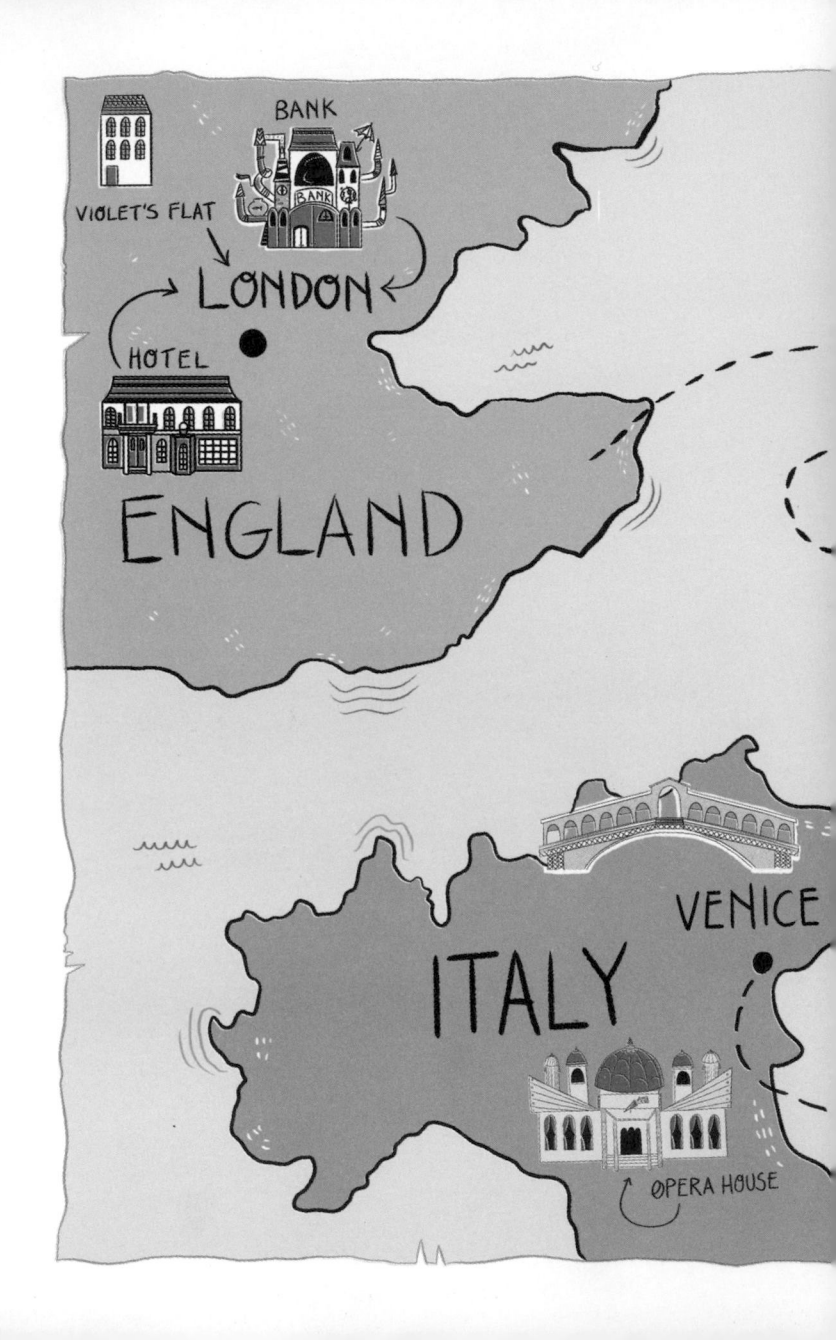

FOR PHOEBE – HW

FOR CALLUM – BM

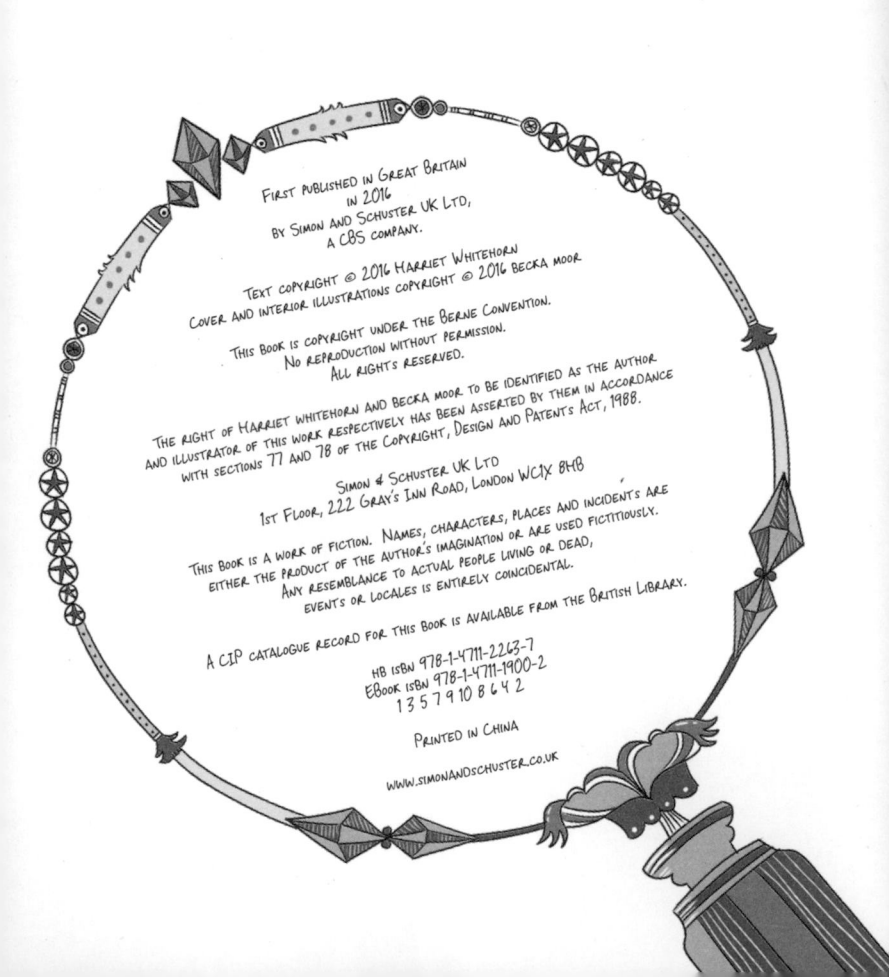

First published in Great Britain
in 2016
by Simon and Schuster UK Ltd,
A CBS company.

Text copyright © 2016 Harriet Whitehorn
Cover and interior illustrations copyright © 2016 Becka Moor

The right of Harriet Whitehorn and Becka Moor to be identified as the author
and illustrator of this work respectively has been asserted by them in accordance
with sections 77 and 78 of the Copyright, Design and Patents Act, 1988.

Simon & Schuster UK Ltd
1st Floor, 222 Gray's Inn Road, London WC1X 8HB

A CIP catalogue record for this book is available from the British Library.

HB ISBN 978-1-4711-2263-7
EBook ISBN 978-1-4711-1900-2
1 3 5 7 9 10 8 6 4 2

Printed in China

WWW.SIMONANDSCHUSTER.CO.UK

This is a story about Violet Remy-Robinson.

Violet lives with her mother, Camille, and her father, Benedict, as well as her cat, Pudding and her cockatoo, the Maharani. Violet is a brilliant at two things – climbing and playing poker. She lives in a flat that backs onto a large garden, called a communal garden, because all the people who live near Violet share it. Violet's special friends who live around the garden are Rose, with whom she also goes to school, and Art, who lives with his great aunt, an eccentric lady called Dee Dee Derota.

Violet is always on the look-out for adventure, and she, together with Rose and Art, have solved two previous mysteries – the theft of a jewel that belonged to Dee Dee, named the Pearl of the Orient, and also the kidnapping of the cockatoo who now lives with her, the Maharani. In both of these cases she had a little help from a policeman called PC Green (very little, Violet would say, although PC Green may say differently). Now, in this story, Violet and her friends go on an adventure to Italy and Italians love ice cream. So, what better way to introduce you to everyone than telling you what their favourite ice-cream flavour is!

VIOLET

VIOLET'S FAVOURITE IS MINT CHOC CHIP.

CAMILLE

CAMILLE DEFINITELY LIKES A DARK, RICH CHOCOLATE BEST.

BENEDICT

BENEDICT WAS TORN BETWEEN RASPBERRY RIPPLE AND PISTACHIO.

GODFATHER JOHNNY

THE ONLY FLAVOUR ICE CREAM JOHNNY LIKES IS RUM AND RAISIN.

ROSE

ROSE LOVES PLAIN OLD STRAWBERRY ICE CREAM.

ART

ART LIKES SORBETS AND LEMON IS HIS FAVOURITE,

LA BELLISSIMA

LA BELLISSIMA DOESN'T EAT ICE CREAM BECAUSE IT'S BAD FOR YOUR SINGING VOICE.

GRAND-MÈRE

GRAND-MÈRE ALWAYS CHOSES BANANA.

DEE DEE DEROTA

DEE DEE LOVES TUTTI FRUTTI.

PC GREEN

PC GREEN FOUND IT ALMOST IMPOSSIBLE TO CHOOSE BUT DECIDED HE REALLY COULDN'T LIVE WITHOUT CARAMEL.

1
SOMETHING EXCITING

This book starts with a letter.

It was a summery Saturday morning at the beginning of July and all was peaceful in the Remy-Robinson household. The sun was flooding through the open sitting room windows, shining down on Violet, who was lying on the floor doing her maths homework, with surprisingly little complaint. Her mother, Camille, sat nearby, curled up in a chair, reading a newspaper. The Maharani, Violet's cockatoo, was perched on the back

of Camille's chair (apparently reading the newspaper too) and Pudding the cat was snoozing on the window sill.

There was the sound of a gentle plop from the hall as the post fell onto the doormat, and a few moments later, Benedict, Violet's father, strode in clutching a letter.

'Well, something very exciting has happened,' he announced and everyone turned to look at him.

'What?' Violet and her mother asked at the same time.

'Johnny has inherited a boat.'

Johnny was Violet's godfather and Benedict's oldest friend.

'A boat? That is exciting!' said Violet.

'What sort of boat?' Camille asked.

'It is a smallish, rather old sailing boat,' Benedict said. 'It belonged to Johnny's Great Uncle Marmaduke. I remember we had a very funny holiday on it when I was about thirteen because there were at least eight of us squashed into it!' He smiled at the thought. 'It had an Italian name, I think . . . I can't remember what.' He paused, wracking his brains. 'Anyway, Johnny has written from Corfu in Greece, where the boat is currently moored. As it's the start of Violet's school

holiday next week, he's invited us to go on a sailing adventure with him.'

Violet gasped. 'You are, of course, invited, my love,' Benedict said to Camille, 'but the boat will be quite basic with no running water, so perhaps . . . an adventure like this is not really your thing.'

'I agree,' Camille said and gave a delicate shiver at the thought of being stuck on a sailing boat for more than an afternoon. 'But when Violet finishes school we only have two weeks before we have to meet Grand-mère in Venice and I have also promised Dee Dee that we will look after Art while she is visiting her sister in the Isle of Wight. I have already booked a tutor to give them some extra maths and French lessons.'

Benedict and Violet's eyes met and silently she begged him to change her mother's mind.

'Well, this is just an idea,' Benedict said carefully. 'But maybe I could take Art and Violet to Corfu and then we could sail up to meet you and Grand-mère in Venice. I'll make sure we talk a bit of French on the boat and Johnny is brilliant at maths. Think how delighted Grand-mère will be to see Johnny; you know how keen she is on him.'

Camille looked unsure.

Violet could contain herself no longer. 'Oh, please, please, please, please. I'll be so good, I'll work so hard, I'll do anything, just please can we go?' She looked pleadingly at her mother.

'Well, I'll need to talk to Dee Dee,' Camille said. 'She may not be happy about Art going, or he may not want to.'

Violet didn't think that was very likely. Art was even keener on adventures than she was.

'And don't forget Rose is coming to Venice with us so you should ask her too. Otherwise she will have to travel out to Venice on her own with me and Grand-mère.'

Violet could hardly contain her excitement. 'Yes, please. It would be such fun if Rose could come too!'

Camille smiled. 'Okay, we will talk to Rose and her parents as well. Now, speaking of Venice, Grand-mère rang yesterday to say that La Bellissima is singing at the Opera House while we are there and she wanted to know if she should book tickets.'

'Who's La Bellissima?' Violet asked.

'She is a very famous Italian opera singer,' Camille explained. 'Look, there is a picture of her in the newspaper. She's holding her pet tortoise.'

'That's what Johnny's boat is called!' Benedict exclaimed. 'The Italian word for tortoise. Is it *tartufo, tartortu* . . . or something like that.'

'*Taratuga*,' Violet said. Italian was one of Violet's many after-school activities.

'Yes! *Il Taratuga*. Well done, Violet!'

Violet beamed as she examined the photo of La Bellissima. She was a very glamorous looking lady, who was cuddling up to a tortoise which seemed to be covered in diamonds.

'Doesn't it hurt the tortoise having all those diamonds stuck on its shell?' Violet asked.

'Probably,' Camille answered. 'But La Bellissima has started a horrible trend and now everyone wants a diamond-encrusted tortoise.'

'I don't think that anyone

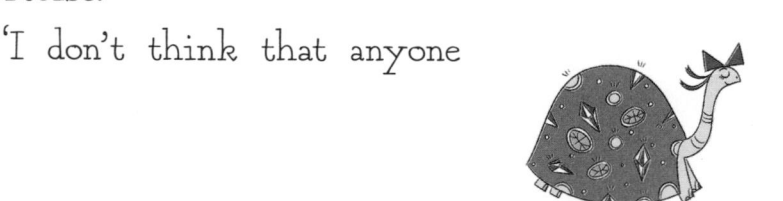

really knows whether it does hurt the tortoises,' Benedict said. 'But they were saying on the news that the craze has led to a world shortage of tortoises and they are now fetching the most astronomical prices. Apparently people are smuggling them around the world, mostly taking them to Amsterdam where they get stuck full of diamonds.'

'Oh, that sounds horrible!' said Violet. She loved tortoises and would regularly go off into the countryside near where her grandmother lived in France to look for them. You may not know this, but tortoises live in the wild all over southern Europe, so you can see them when you are out for a walk, like you would a fox or a rabbit in England.

'Well, anyway' Camille said. 'Grand-mère is a huge fan of La Bellissima as a singer and I know she would like to see her perform. So who else would like to go?'

Violet couldn't imagine anything more dull so she said no thank you.

'Why don't you go with your mother?' Benedict suggested quickly, obviously as keen as Violet not to go to the Opera. 'Johnny and I can go to the casino instead.'

Camille raised an eyebrow. 'And who will look after the children?'

'Of course, silly me, I meant, Johnny and I can look after the children.'

'Excellent. I'll tell Grand-mère to buy two tickets. Now, Violet, shall we just nip across the garden and see if Dee Dee and Art, and Rose and her parents are in?'

2
IL TARATUGA

Ten days later, Violet found herself sitting in the back of a taxi with Art, bumping down the white, cobbled streets of Corfu Town towards the port, trying not to listen to her father practising his terrible Greek with the taxi driver and fizzing with excitement to get to the boat.

Of course, when they had gone to see Dee Dee to ask about Art joining the trip, Art had started jumping around with over-excitement at the thought of a voyage on a boat. Dee Dee, who was not the strictest of great aunts, had said to Camille: 'I think we had better let them go, don't you, darlin'? It sounds so much more fun than extra French and maths.' So Lavinia, Dee Dee's life-organiser, immediately went and bought some clothes for Art that would be suitable to wear on the boat and, much to Violet's amusement, Art had arrived at the airport with a huge suitcase, wearing a white linen sailor suit and looking very embarrassed.

'Doesn't he look just edible?' Dee Dee had exclaimed as Art scowled. And now, in the fierce Greek heat, Art was bright red in the face, his white suit completely crumpled from the flight.

Rose, however, was not in the taxi with her two friends. Camille and Violet had been to ask her to come on the trip too as soon as they'd left Dee Dee's flat, but Rose's response hadn't been quite the same as Art's. Poor Rose! Part of her wanted to go, because what could be more fun than an adventure with your two best friends? But the other, larger, part of her, couldn't think of anything worse. Just last year she had been on a cross-channel ferry in bad weather and it had made her horribly sick. The thought of being on a tiny boat for over a week, possibly running into storms, big waves

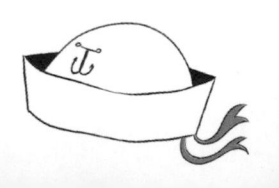

and high winds was too much. And what about not being able to have a bath? Would there even be a proper loo? It all sounded very stressful, so Rose gabbled that she was sorry but she couldn't possibly come because she had to go to an incredibly important ballet summer camp before they went to Venice. Which was true. Or, at least, partly true; she was doing a couple of extra ballet lessons but they weren't really important. And, of course, she reassured Camille, she didn't mind travelling just with her and Violet's grandmother on the train. Trains were nice orderly things, unlike boats, and Rose trusted Camille entirely because

LANDLUBBERS

SICK BAG

she was incredibly organised, very kind and was sure to bring lots of delicious food for the journey.

So, it was only Violet and Art for the first part of the trip, although they were both very much looking forward to seeing Rose in a couple of weeks' time.

The taxi dropped them at the port, and the three of them went to find *Il Taratuga*. At last they spotted the boat. It was right at the end of a quay with a tanned and happy-looking Johnny on its deck.

Il Taratuga was exactly as Violet had

imagined her. She was about as long as two cars and made of wood, with a bright orange sail that was neatly rolled up. As Johnny and Benedict greeted each other, Violet and Art scampered down some little rickety stairs to a small, cosy sitting area and tiny kitchen below deck. Next to them were two weeny cabins and the whole inside was lined in wood. Violet thought it was very like being inside a tree. They came back on deck to find Benedict and Johnny standing over Art's enormous suitcase.

'Art, my boy,' Johnny said firmly. 'I think some surgery is needed.' Art was puzzled, but didn't object as Johnny opened the suitcase to

reveal a smart navy blue blazer, several crisp shirts, trousers, cravats, a naval cap and a pair of shiny leather shoes. 'I think that this is a suitcase for a different sort of boat.'

Johnny disappeared into the cabin for a moment, returning with a large pair of scissors. Art looked alarmed.

'Is it going to hurt?' he stuttered.

'Only a little,' Johnny replied and, before Art could object, Johnny had cut the legs off two pairs of trousers, turning them into shorts. Then he trimmed the arms off three shirts, making them short-sleeved. He found some swimming trunks and a pair of flip-flops in the case and handed the small pile to Art,

"SNIP SNIP"

"SNIP"

who grinned broadly, delighted.

'Can I go and get changed?' he asked.

'Definitely,' Johnny replied. 'But I think I might have to have this hat.' Johnny tried to cram the naval cap onto his head. It didn't fit.

'What a shame,' he said. 'You had better hang onto that. Looks like you're the captain now. Hurry and change, Art. We should have a quick sailing lesson before we set off tomorrow. Who's good at tying knots?'

Later, when the light was fading from the sky, they all walked to a bustling restaurant in town. They sat outside at a wobbly table and ate all sorts of delicious food – little fried fish, great big beans in tomato sauce, crunchy triangular cheese pies and moussaka, with yoghurt and honey to finish. And between mouthfuls, they pored over a map, plotting their route from Corfu to Venice. This is what they decided:

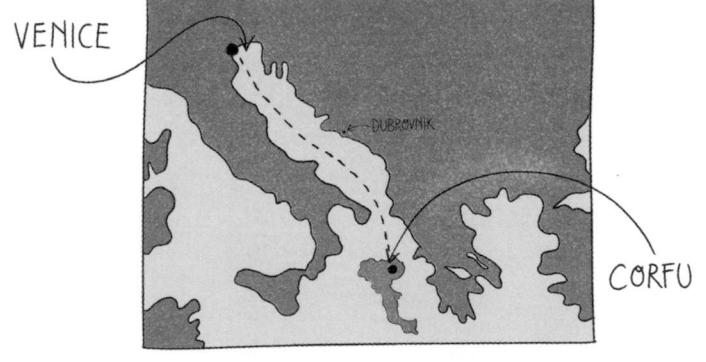

They walked back to the boat, full of yummy food and excited about their plans. But as they neared the quay, they heard loud opera music.

'Oh no,' groaned Johnny. 'Not again. Every night so far, the Italian captain of the old tourist boat next door plays opera as he eats his supper. I call him Mr Jolly, partly because it's the name of his boat in Italian and partly. . . well, you'll see why. '

As they got closer they could see the tourist boat. She was as old as *Il Taratuga* but instead of being a pretty sailing boat, she was a large, lumbering motorboat. Her white-and-blue paint must have once been very smart, though now it was peeling everywhere, and a

jaunty sign saying, 'Day Trips' must have been enticing to tourists, but now it just looked rather sad. A very serious-looking man sat on the deck at a small table. With a napkin tucked into his shirt, he was slowly eating a large bowl of spaghetti and meatballs, while the music blared from an old-fashioned record player next to the table.

'*Buona Sera*,' Johnny and Benedict greeted him politely.

'*Buona Sera*,' the man responded mournfully.

'When does the music go off?' Benedict asked Johnny in a whisper.

'I'm afraid he still has pudding, coffee and a cigar to go. About an hour, I should think.'

'Well, it's time we went to bed. It's been a long day and we've got to be up at dawn to set off,' Benedict said. 'Everyone will just have to put a pillow over their heads.'

Violet was sharing a cabin with Benedict.

'I'll never get to sleep with that racket going on,' he sighed, climbing up to the top bunk, but barely five minutes later, his snores were drowning out the opera.

Great, thought Violet, though she too dropped off to sleep not long after.

3
HOW VERY MYSTERIOUS

Maybe it was the swaying of the boat, or a mosquito buzzing by her ear, but something woke Violet just a few hours later. It was very hot and still. She sat up and gazed through the tiny porthole in her cabin at the moon, which hung low in the sky, sending a silvery path shimmering across the water. It was so beautiful that she wanted to go and have a better look. Her father was breathing deeply in his sleep on the bunk above her. *What would be the harm*, Violet thought, *if I went*

on deck for a moment? She crept silently up the steps.

Outside there was a slight breeze, which was deliciously cooling, and Violet lay on her back looking at the stars. She had been studying constellations at school and was searching for the Big Dipper when she smelled a strong waft of cigar smoke. Who was smoking? She flipped over on her tummy and crawled to the edge of the boat to have a look. Just a few metres away sat Mr Jolly, smoking a cigar in the dark.

He was facing the harbour and looked as if he was waiting for someone. Violet was curious; who could he be meeting at this time of night?

She heard the gentle creaking of the bicycle before she saw it, as it had no lights on. *Someone obviously doesn't want to be seen*, Violet thought. The rider was a boy of about twelve, who exchanged whispered greetings with Mr Jolly, before handing over a large flat box that had been strapped to the back of his bicycle. Mr Jolly looked inside, nodded, then handed a pile of banknotes to the boy. Quickly, the boy rode away and then Mr Jolly picked up

the box and went below deck.

How very mysterious, Violet thought, as she crept back to her bunk. *What on earth could have been in that box?*

The following morning, all was quiet on Mr Jolly's boat as Johnny steered them out of the dock.

Violet told Art about what she had seen the night before.

'Well, he must be a smuggler,' he said knowingly.

'Of course!' Violet exclaimed. 'What do you think was in the box?'

Art was about to reply but Johnny started shouting things like, 'Hoist the main sail!' and 'Come around!' and there was no more time for chatting, as she and Art scurried back and forth across the boat, tying and untying ropes.

The wind was strong and Il Taratuga zipped along so that soon they were out in the open sea. A school of dolphins appeared and swam with them for a while, much to everyone's delight. 'It's a good omen,' Johnny announced happily.

This story is not really about Violet and Art's time on *Il Taratuga*, so I'm afraid we will have to skip forward a little bit.

Several things of note did happen over the next week as they wended their way up the coast.

Art fell overboard ten times.

Violet beat Johnny and Benedict at poker nine times.

Johnny called them all 'useless land-lubbers' eight times.

Art caught seven magnificent fish.

They slept out on deck under the stars six nights running.

Violet and Art saw five shooting stars each.

They made a fire and cooked their supper on a deserted island on four evenings.

One day they saw three octopuses while they were swimming.

The boat nearly drifted away twice because no one had thought to secure the anchor properly.

And they spoke French and did a bit of maths once.

4
SMUGGLERS AHOY

One week and a lot of fun later, Violet was standing patiently in the middle of a mountain of shopping bags as Johnny chose some cheese and salami in a little grocery shop near the harbour in Dubrovnik. There was a rack of foreign newspapers beside her and a headline in English caught her eye.

LA BELLISSIMA'S SELL-OUT EUROPEAN TOUR CONTINUES IN VENICE ~ TICKETS CHANGE HANDS FOR RECORD PRICES.

Grand-mère hadn't been able to get tickets to see the opera star, much to her disappointment, and it didn't sound as if she would have a chance of getting any now - oh dear! Violet would have read more, but the small article below looked more interesting:

POLICE STRUGGLE TO SMASH DIAMOND SMUGGLING RING.

ITALIAN POLICE HAVE BEEN TIPPED OFF ABOUT A GANG OF DIAMOND SMUGGLERS WHO ARE BRINGING THE GEMS UP FROM NORTH AFRICA AND INTO EUROPE THROUGH ITALY AND SPAIN. SO FAR THEY HAVE NO DEFINITE LEADS, BUT POLICE SUSPECT THAT THEY MAY BE TRAVELLING BY BOAT. THE FINAL DESTINATION OF THE DIAMONDS IS LIKELY TO BE THE DUTCH CITY OF AMSTERDAM, WHERE...

'Right, we're done,' Johnny announced, handing over some money to the elderly shop keeper. 'Are you ready to go?' he asked Violet.

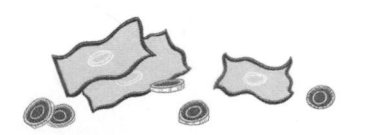

Violet nodded, although she still had one eye on the newspaper article while Johnny loaded them both up with the shopping bags.

It felt strange to be back on land. Violet was so used to the rocking of the boat that the ground almost seemed to be moving beneath her as they made their way through the crowds of tourists and locals out for an early evening stroll. They had arranged to meet Art and Benedict in a café and as they drew nearer they spotted them drinking milkshakes and writing postcards.

'Excellent!' Benedict exclaimed at the sight of the bags. 'There's enough food to keep us going all the way to Venice. I just spoke to Camille and she sends her love, especially to you, Violet. Dee Dee's sister is not feeling very well, so Dee Dee wants to spend longer with her and she has asked if Art can stay with us in Venice.'

Violet beamed at her friend, delighted he'd be along for the whole holiday.

'It did sound as if your mother was feeling a bit nervous about the journey. For a start, she has to bring the Maharani because Norma is away and Lavinia is allergic to birds (or so she says), so she can only look after Pudding. Anyway, Camille leaves with Rose the day after tomorrow. They stop in Paris for a night before travelling on to the south of France where they meet Grand-mère and Alphonse and get the train to Venice. Oh dear, I hope Grand-mère behaves herself.'

'Who on earth is Alphonse? I thought Grand-mère only had eyes for me,' Johnny said with a cheeky grin.

Violet laughed. 'Alphonse is her really naughty French bulldog. Grand-mère refuses to tell him off and whenever he does something dreadful she just says, "I'm sorry, he cannot help it, he is just a puppy", when he's five years old! He's so spoilt that he has a different little coat for every day of the week!'

Violet was about to tell Art a funny story about Alphonse when she saw a familiar figure walking nearby.

'Look! It's Mr Jolly!' she whispered to Art.

'The smuggler?' Art replied. 'We should watch him for further evidence.'

Luckily, Mr Jolly sat down on a bench opposite, so they were able to keep an eye on him. Only a few minutes later, a man holding a large box sat next to him. The man placed the box carefully on the bench between them. At first, Mr Jolly totally ignored him, then Art and Violet watched as he pulled an envelope out of his pocket and placed it casually on top of the box. The other man took the envelope and strolled off. Mr Jolly picked up the box and walked away too.

Art and Violet looked at each other, eyes wide.

'That was straight out of a spy movie!!' Art exclaimed.

'I've just seen a newspaper story about a gang of diamond smugglers. Maybe he's one of them! We should follow him!' Violet cried

'Follow who?' Benedict interrupted.

Violet sensed that her father might not see the enormous importance of following Mr Jolly, so she did something, dear reader, you must never do. She told a large fib!

'Oh, I've just remembered that I promised to send my chess tutor a postcard . . . he wanted to follow our trip.'

'Can't you send him one from Venice?' Johnny asked.

'No. He, um . . . specifically wanted one from Dubrovnik. He has a great aunt who lived here.' The fib expanded.

Benedict looked sceptical, but handed Violet a few coins. 'Well, meet us back at the boat, but be quick, I don't want you wandering around for a long time on your own.'

'Of course!' Violet cried and she and Art sped off after Mr Jolly.

Mr Jolly was quite a large man, but he walked surprisingly quickly. It took Violet and Art a few minutes to catch up with him as he weaved his way nimbly through the crowds, carrying the box ahead of him like a tea tray. He looked as if he was heading towards the harbour, but then he stopped abruptly and went into a café instead. They watched Mr Jolly through the café's large window as he sat down at the bar, placing the box carefully on the neighbouring stool, and ordered a drink.

'What shall we do now?' Art asked.

Violet thought for a moment. 'I think you should stay outside, ready to follow him in case he makes off again. I'll go in and see if I can get a look into the box.'

Jangling the coins her father had given her, Violet marched straight to the bar, next to Mr Jolly and asked for a Coca-Cola. Mr Jolly took absolutely no notice of her. The

box was very close, and as Violet began to sip her drink, she could see there was a small gap between the lid and the sides. If only she could take a peek! Violet was about to pretend to drop something so she could try and look in the box when Art came in, distracting her for a moment. He flicked his eyes towards the street and Violet followed his gaze to see Johnny and Benedict walking past the café. She swivelled away from the window.

'Coca-Cola for you too?' the barman asked Art in English.

'Yes, please,' Art replied.

'Here, come and sit next to your friend,' Mr Jolly said. He spoke English with a very strong Italian accent, and moved to pick up the box.

'No, no, please don't worry!' Violet exclaimed. But before she could stop him he had lifted it to the bar stool on his other side.

What to do now? Violet and Art were both thinking as they sucked their drinks noisily through the straws. Violet had just decided that she needed to create a distraction when Mr Jolly got up, finished his drink, threw some coins on the bar and, asking the barman to watch his box, he made his way to the telephone at the back of the café, next to the entrance to the toilet.

'See if you can look in the box,' Violet

whispered to Art and hopped off her stool.

She wandered towards the toilet and tried the door. Pretending it was occupied, Violet desperately tried not to seem as if she was listening to every word of Mr Jolly's phone conversation. It was all in Italian but, as we know, Violet's Italian was pretty good. This is what she heard:

'Yes, Boss, yes. No problems so far. All is good for next Friday night. We arrive that morning at about eleven and I will come straight to you with the goods. Yes, Boss, yes. See you in Venice.'

Violet was a-quiver with excitement - it was Friday today so he must mean in a week's time. *Il Taratuga* would have reached Venice by then too. When she was sure he had finished she made a great play of trying the door to the toilet again and it miraculously opening. But Mr Jolly didn't appear to notice and when she came out of the toilet, he was gone.

'Did you see in the box?' Violet asked Art as she walked back to the bar.

'Not really but I thought I saw something gleaming through the gap.'

Violet gasped. 'Like a diamond?!'

'Maybe,' Art said, unsure.

Violet was beside herself. 'I bet he's part of

the diamond smuggling gang. Come on, let's follow him. He's probably going back to his boat. I'll tell you on the way all about his telephone conversation.'

They paid for their drinks and headed for the harbour. There was no sign of Mr Jolly himself, but they saw his boat moored not far from *Il Taratuga*. The pair walked slowly past the boat, desperately sneaking glances to see if they could see anything. Something caught Violet's eye.

'What's that?' she whispered to Art, pointing at a small brown thing on deck that appeared to be moving.

'I think . . . it's a tortoise!' Art replied,

craning his neck to see.

'Oh, how sweet! I love tortoises,' Violet cried, forgetting all about smuggling and being secretive for a moment. 'That's what Johnny should have – a ship's tortoise. Come on, let's go and see it!' And she bounded up the gang plank onto the boat.

Unfortunately, at that moment, Mr Jolly came out on deck.

'Well, I don't see why he had to get so cross with me,' Violet complained to Art, as they walked back to *Il Taratuga* a few minutes later. 'I was only being nice to his tortoise. Honestly!'

5
VENICE

Il Taratuga sailed into Venice at dawn on Tuesday morning, and after they had moored the boat, Violet, Art, Benedict and Johnny walked through the maze of narrow, empty streets to the *Pensione Renaldo*, the small hotel where the Remy-Robinsons stayed every year. Violet was so excited to see her mother and Grand-mère that she was practically skipping and Art was wide-eyed with amazement at Venice. 'I can't believe how cool it is here,' he said. 'Boats instead of cars!'

Art and Violet charged through the hotel entrance into the little courtyard garden and bumped straight into Camille, who had been waiting eagerly for their arrival.

'Oh, my goodness me, it's so lovely to see you!' Camille said as she hugged Violet tight to her. 'Perhaps you had just better go and jump in the bath before you see Grand-mère,' she added as she stood back and took in their appearance.

Violet's skin was very tanned and her hair was still in the same plaits that Camille had carefully done before she went to the airport, but her hair was now so full of salt that the plaits stuck out like Pippi Longstocking's. Art

was one big freckle and his red hair had been bleached to a coppery colour by the sun and sticking on end like a loo brush.

'Too late,' grinned Violet. 'Grand-mère!' she cried, running towards an elderly lady who had just come into the courtyard.

'Who is this savage?' Grand-mère said, and brandished her walking stick like a sword at Violet.

'It's me, Grand-mère!' Violet laughed.

'It cannot be. My granddaughter is a neat, clean child and you are a filthy urchin!' Grand-mère exclaimed, trying to hide a grin.

'It *is* me!'

At that moment, Alphonse appeared and

charged straight towards Violet, tail wagging. He was closely followed by the Maharani who shrieked, 'Vi-let! Vi-let!'

'Well, the animals seem to recognise you,' Grand-mère said and, using her walking stick as a hook, she pulled Violet to her, peering at her over the top of her glasses.

Violet launched herself at Grand-mère for a hug.

'Non, non, non, Violet,' she shrieked, wrinkling her nose. 'You smell like an old dog. Go and have a bath and hurry or I will eat all the croissants. You too, young man,' she added, looking at Art. 'Let us become properly acquainted once you are clean.'

Violet and Art went to their rooms, had the fastest baths imaginable and sprinted back down to breakfast. A long table sat in the shade of a lemon tree, piled high with croissants, cake, bread and jam and pots of coffee and tea. Everyone was sitting around it. Johnny was busy making Grand-mère shriek with laughter, while she fed Alphonse bits of cake. The dog was sitting on his own special chair with the Maharani sitting on the back, gazing

adoringly at him. Happy to be together again, Camille and Benedict were holding hands. Violet took a very dim view of any form of soppiness so she gave them her sternest frown. And of course Rose was there. Rose grinned with delight when she saw Violet and Art. Violet was bursting to tell her all about the smuggler, but as they sat down Camille said, 'I should think Rose is very pleased to see you both. We had quite an eventful journey on the way here.'

'Oh, really?' Benedict asked. 'Come on, tell us why.'

Camille lowered her voice.

'Well, there were several minor incidents,

but by far the worst bit was when we got on the wrong train. Grand-mère pulled the emergency brake as we were leaving the station.'

Benedict smothered his laughter. Camille allowed herself a giggle.

'Poor Rose. It was very embarrassing, wasn't it, *chérie*?'

Rose nodded, biting her lip. 'There was a lot of shouting,' she said.

Grand-mère's ears pricked up.

'Are you talking about that silly guard on the train? What a fuss! How can he have expected me to stay on the wrong train? Trains can reverse, you know. Anyway, he was quite rude until I explained about my work in the

French Resistance during the war. That shut him up,' she said with satisfaction.

'Rose, you have all my sympathy,' Benedict managed to say between guffaws. 'I have had similar experiences travelling with Grand-mère.'

'You know, Rose,' Grand-mère said, not unkindly. 'Sometimes in life, if you are going somewhere you don't want to go, you have to be brave and pull the emergency brake.'

Signora Renaldo, the owner of the hotel, appeared with large bowls of hot chocolate for Rose, Art and Violet. With her was a young woman with a kind face, long black curly hair and large brown eyes. She was wearing lots of silver jewellery and a flowery, floaty dress.

'This is my niece, Elena,' Signora Renaldo said, introducing her. 'She is helping me for the rest of the summer. She has just come back from travelling in India.'

'Hello,' Elena said shyly.

She seems nice, thought Violet, glancing around the table. Everyone was smiling at Elena, except Johnny, who looked like he'd seen a ghost, only he wasn't pale, but very pink in the face.

'What's the matter with Uncle Johnny?' Violet whispered to her mother.

'Oh, nothing,' Camille whispered back.

Rose was listening. 'I think he thinks Elena is pretty,' she explained to Violet in a whisper.

'Oh,' Violet replied. 'Well, if he keeps looking like that, she's going to think he's pretty silly!'

6
THE DIAMOND BAKLAVA SMUGGLERS

'Children, I have to collect Alphonse from the beauty parlour and I have some little errands I would like you to do for me – just a few things from the shops on the square around the corner,' Grand-mère announced the following day. It was seven in the evening and Rose, Art and Violet had all had their baths after a day at the beach, and while the grown-ups were getting ready for supper, they were playing cards at a table in the courtyard and discussing Mr Jolly. Violet and Art had filled Rose in on every detail. The Maharani was with them, looking around longingly for Alphonse. The children sprang up immediately because, however fun cards were, an unaccompanied shopping trip was even better.

Grand-mère produced a list from her handbag.

'Now, Violet, concentrate. I need you to go to the pharmacy and then the stationers, and then . . . ' She gave Violet a handful of notes with a wink, saying, 'Don't buy ice cream with the change and ruin your appetites. Be back in twenty minutes. Dinner is at seven-thirty sharp and we don't want to keep Signora Renaldo waiting.'

The children charged out into the busy street and ran up to the Square. Clutching the list, they made their way around the shops until they were laden with little bags and packages. Art counted the change.

'Just enough for three small cones,' he said, as they strolled into the ice cream shop.

I don't know if you have ever been into an Italian ice cream shop but they are one of the best places ever invented. Rows and rows of zingy coloured ice cream are laid out for you to drool over, with exciting names such as *zuppa inglese*, *frutti di bosca* and *stracciatella*.

Violet went through her usual debate of

whether she should have melon or caramel or maybe even chocolate. Then, as always, she decided to stick to her favourite – mint choc chip. The shop was crowded inside, mostly because there was a man ordering the largest ice cream you can imagine in a mixture of terrible Italian and English. Everyone was rolling their eyes and sighing as he stumbled slowly on,

'Er *tutti frutti* next, *chocalato*, strawberry and a bit of *minta, per favore* and that's it.' Finally he handed a note over to the girl behind the counter and the whole shop breathed a sigh of relief.

All the children stared at his back.

'Isn't that . . . ?' Rose began, in an amazed voice.

'Yes I think it is . . . ' Art replied.,

'PC GREEN!' Violet cried.

The man spun around, nearly sending his ice cream flying.

'Violet! Rose! Art ! What on earth are you doing here?'

'We're on holiday. What are you doing here? And why are you dressed as an Italian policeman?' Violet asked.

PC Green was looking extremely smart in a pale blue shirt, navy blue trousers with a red stripe down the side, a cap and very, very shiny black boots.

'I am an Italian policeman!' he cried, totally over excited. 'For a whole month. There was an exchange at work and the Chief Inspector nominated me above everyone else. In fact, he seemed very keen for me to come and kept cracking jokes about having a peaceful summer without me.'

The children were now at the front of the queue and ordered their ice creams – mint choc chip for Violet, strawberry for Rose and lemon sorbet for Art.

They wandered outside as PC

Green continued, hardly able to contain himself. 'I am living the dream!' he gushed. 'Not only do I get to wear this smart uniform and eat ice cream every day, but you'll never guess what my main duty is this week?'

'Giving tourists directions?'

'No!'

'Fishing people out of canals?'

'No! Looking after La Bellissima!' They all looked so amazed that he began to explain, 'You must have heard of her? She's a very famous opera singer. There are posters of her everywhere. Look there's one – isn't she really, really beautiful?' He pointed to a huge billboard poster of La Bellissima pouting like

a duck with a blonde wig on.

'Yes, I know who she is, it's just—' Violet was about to say that she couldn't believe PC Green had been trusted to look after someone like La Bellissima, when Art interrupted.

'They've trusted you to look after an actual famous person? That's amazing.'

'I know,' the policeman agreed. 'I couldn't believe it either. And honestly, chaps, she is SO lovely. Not only beautiful on the outside, but on the inside too.' He sighed.

'PC Green, it's actually very lucky you're here.' Violet said. 'Art and I have been tracking a criminal, all the way from Corfu. He's definitely a smuggler who is hoping to pull off a big deal here in Venice on Friday night. I suspect that he is part of the diamond smuggling ring that has been in the newspapers.'

'Wow,' PC Green said. 'Good work. Tell me more.'

And so Violet told him all about Mr Jolly and the boxes.

'The boxes sound a bit big for diamonds, don't they?' he said when she'd finished.

Rose stepped in.

'Maybe they are hiding the diamonds in something else,' she said. 'That's what smugglers often do, isn't it?'

PC Green nodded. 'You are quite right, Rose. I wonder what they could be using?'

They all thought for a moment and then PC Green almost shouted,

'I know! What about baklava? That's what I'd smuggle from Greece to Italy, diamonds or no diamonds. I love that stuff – sticky and nutty and delicious. The Diamond Baklava Smugglers – you could really be onto something here. Now smugglers are usually VERY dangerous, so you had better leave it to me to investigate. You let me know if you see him again. Oh, look, here's your lovely mother, Violet. Uh oh, she looks a bit cross, are you lot supposed to be somewhere else?'

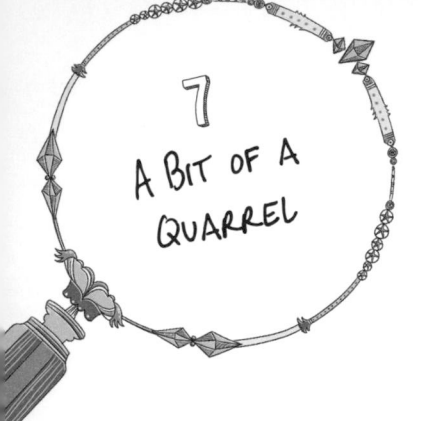

7
A BIT OF A QUARREL

A couple of days later, on Friday morning, Violet, Art and Rose were lying on the deck of *Il Taratuga* waiting for Mr Jolly to arrive. The waves were lapping gently at the side of the boat, the warm sun was shining and all should have been well, but if you had happened to see their faces you would have thought that something was seriously wrong. Johnny and Elena were at the other end of the boat, talking in low voices.

'Did you really just see them kissing?' Violet whispered to Art.

Art nodded, with an expression on his face as if he had just eaten a chilli-flavoured jellybean when he had expected a strawberry one.

'Yuck, how disgusting!' Violet exclaimed.

'I think it's sweet,' Rose said.

Art and Violet both looked at her in horror.

They would have continued this conversation further had they not then been distracted by a boat slowly chugging into the harbour.

'IT'S MR JOLLY!' Violet cried, brimming with excitement. 'Right on time. Now we just have to follow to him to

find out what's in the boxes. I bet it is diamonds.'

'I've been thinking,' Rose began a little nervously. And she had; in fact, she had hardly slept the night before for worrying. 'PC Green said that diamond smugglers are dangerous—'

'PC Green thinks everyone is a dangerous criminal,' Art interrupted.

'But he's probably right in this case,' Rose protested. 'Why don't we just go and tell PC Green that Mr Jolly's arrived?'

'No way,' Violet replied. 'This is our case! PC Green didn't seem to know how to catch a smuggler anyway.'

'I know but. . .' Rose trailed off.

'Aren't you curious at all?' Violet asked.

'Of course, I just don't think we should try to catch the smugglers on our own,' Rose replied definitely.

'You don't have to if you are too scared,' Violet said, a teeny bit meanly. 'Art and I will manage perfectly well without you.'

'Fine,' Rose replied, feeling hurt. She got up and went to the other side of boat.

Johnny and Elena appeared at that moment, hand in hand. They looked very happy, but Johnny noticed that Rose was on her own.

'I hope there is no fighting going on,' he said. 'Shall we go back to the hotel? Anyone want an ice cream on the way?'

'Yes, please,' Rose said, jumping to her feet. She was feeling hot and sticky and upset and just wanted to be back in the nice, cool hotel.

But Violet had no intention of going back yet. She and Art needed to watch Mr Jolly.

'Can't we stay a bit longer?' she asked. 'Why don't you go back with Rose, and Art and I will come along later?'

Johnny raised one eyebrow at Violet.

'Absolutely not. I can't leave you alone on the boat.'

Violet was about to object, but then she glanced behind Johnny and saw Mr Jolly was now off his boat and loading a stack of

familiar-looking boxes onto a trolley on the quayside. She nudged Art.

'Okay, but let's go now. We'll race you back!' Violet said and sprinted off, with Art hot on her heels.

'Hey, Violet! Art! Slow down!' Johnny called after them.

They did slow down, but only because Mr Jolly had stopped to look at a noticeboard. Then he was off again at his normal brisk pace, pushing the trolley. Violet and Art were so intent on pursuing him that they didn't bother to glance back at Mr Jolly's boat. If they had, they would have noticed a man standing on the deck, watching them.

The man waited for a moment or two until Violet and Art had scampered away, then he slipped off the boat, and followed them through the streets.

At first Mr Jolly took the same route up the busy main street that Violet and Art would have back to the hotel. But then he made a sharp right over a bridge and into an alley.

Violet and Art paused, unsure what

to do. Rose, Elena and Johnny had stopped to talk to some friends of Elena's. Meanwhile, Mr Jolly's head was bobbing out of sight.

'Why don't you follow him and I'll cover for you with the others?' Art suggested.

'I won't be long,' Violet assured Art. 'They'll probably still be chatting by the time I get back.' And she sprinted off down the alley, unaware of the man from Mr Jolly's boat close behind her.

The alley burst into a small square that was dominated on one side by a large, grand building. Mr Jolly was heading towards it. Violet noticed when she got closer that it was plastered in posters of La Bellissima, and sure enough, she could hear the tra-la-la of her famous voice drifting out from inside.

Mr Jolly didn't go in the main entrance, but instead slipped inside a side door marked, *Ingresso degli Artisti.*

Hmmm, thought Violet, *the stage door!* She pushed it open. There was no sign of Mr Jolly. She asked a rather grumpy-looking man behind a desk whether he had seen a man come in and he told her, not very nicely, that she should go and bother someone else.

8
LA BELLISIMA

Violet stomped out into the Square, still observed by the man from Mr Jolly's boat. He was very relieved to see that she hadn't managed to get into the Opera House. He watched her look around and then, to his horror, he saw her march up to a policeman, who happened to be sitting on the edge of a well in the Square, eating an enormous ice cream. She greeted him like an old friend, and then pointed back at the Opera House. The man grabbed an old newspaper from a

bin, casually strolled towards the well and, pretending to read his paper, he listened in on their conversation. The man didn't understand very much English, but hearing the words *La Bellissima* and *Taratuga* was enough to send him into a spin. He quickly dashed off to the stage door. He had to warn his boss and the big boss that this pesky girl was nosying around!

'Johnny's a lucky chap having this boat, what did you call it?' PC Green said, in between licking his ice cream.

'*Il Taratuga*,' Violet replied impatiently. She wanted PC Green to focus on the smugglers but he kept talking about other things, especially

La Bellissima.

'I wonder if my darling La Bellissima likes boats? There's so much to learn about her. . .' PC Green sighed.

'I don't know,' Violet replied. 'PC Green, please focus, what should we do about the smugglers?'

'Well . . .'

'Maybe you could help me get into the Opera House? I think that's where they're storing the jewels.'

'I do know the manager. His name is Luigi,' PC Green replied.

'What's he like? Could he be a smuggler?' Violet asked.

'Well, now you come to mention it, his eyes are terribly close together,' PC Green replied, stroking his chin thoughtfully.

'Come on, let's go and see him,' Violet said.

'Oh, look, here she comes!' cried PC Green rapturously.

And indeed, La Bellissima herself was gliding towards them, a broad smile on her lovely face. Violet was rather amazed, as somehow she had imagined that PC Green had made it all up. And she was also a little overawed to meet someone so famous.

'*Ciao*,' La Bellissima greeted them, her green eyes twinkling. 'Reginald, you must introduce me.'

'This is Violet. I'm great friends with her family in London. We ran into each other a few days ago in that amazing ice cream shop.'

'What a happy coincidence,' La Bellissima replied.

'Yes, isn't it? Violet often helps me with investigations at home, and this time she's managed to find a case all on her own!' Violet had to stop herself from saying something very rude. PC Green went on, 'Violet and her friends are on the trail of a villain, a diamond smuggler, they suspect. Violet thinks she saw him run into the Opera House, and we were about to ask Luigi if we could search the premises. In fact, I wondered if he might be involved.'

'No! Really?' La Bellissima was wide eyed with amazement.

'Well, his eyes are very close together,' PC Green said knowingly.

La Bellissima gasped. 'How clever you are!'

PC Green grinned and blushed.

'Come, you must get on with your search,' La Bellissima said, leading them back to the Opera House. 'I'm afraid you will not be able to look in my dressing room because I need to rest before tonight's performance but I can assure you there are no smugglers in there.' She laughed prettily, showing her very white teeth. 'Violet, since you are such a special friend of Reginald's, who is so dear to me' – she gave PC Green's hand a quick squeeze, making him blush again – 'I would love you to come to see me sing this evening. With your parents or friends, perhaps? It is my last night in Venice. I leave for Amsterdam tonight.'

Violet paused, thinking quickly. She most certainly didn't want to see La Bellissima perform, but it would give her a chance to do more investigation if she didn't find Mr Jolly and the diamonds now. And she knew Grand-mère would be thrilled. So Violet thanked La Bellissima and said she would love to come.

'*Bravissimo*!' La Bellissima replied, as they reached the stage door. 'I am delighted to help.

I will leave some tickets at the box office for you. Now I must go, but it was delightful to meet you, Violet.' And, after giving PC Green a big kiss, she sashayed off.

'Isn't she just the loveliest person in the world?' PC Green sighed, looking longingly after her.

Violet paused for a moment. There was something that she didn't like about La Bellissima, but she couldn't quite put her finger on it, and she didn't want to be unkind to PC Green so she said politely, 'She does seem very nice.'

'I'm going to let you into a little secret,' he whispered. 'I'm going to ask her to marry me.

Tonight. During the interval. I've even got my great-grandmother's engagement ring to give her. Do you think she'll say yes?'

Violet wasn't sure how to reply, but happily she was saved by PC Green's radio crackling into life.

'*Una ragazza inglese manca.*'

The policeman looked puzzled, and now it was Violet's turn to go red. 'Um, PC Green, I think that's about me: "An English girl is missing".'

'Oh, Violet, it's always you. How do you say "I've found her and will take her home shortly" in Italian?'

'*Lo l'ho trovato e porterò a casa presto.*'

PC Green repeated the words into the radio.

'*Brava, Brava,*' said the crackly radio voice.

'Excellent,' PC Green said to himself. 'That'll make up for when I crashed the speedboat. Now let's just have a quick look around the Opera House and then I'll get you home.'

Violet had to admit that Luigi, the manager of the Opera House, did have eyes that were rather close together, but he seemed nice and not at all like a criminal mastermind to her. He certainly wasn't alarmed by the thought of them searching the Opera House, as long as they didn't disturb La Bellissima. He seemed a little scared of the opera singer, Violet thought.

But, apart from Mr Jolly's trolley, which had been left by the stairs going up to La

Bellissima's dressing room, they found nothing. No boxes, no Mr Jolly, no diamonds. The doorman, who had been so rude to Violet, was suddenly very charming now that PC Green was with her, but he said he hadn't seen anyone arrive with boxes.

As PC Green left her at the entrance to the hotel, Violet's disappointment at not catching the smugglers turned to nerves, as she was sure she was about to get a huge telling off from her parents for running off alone. She went into the courtyard, ready to be shouted at. Art was waiting for her.

'What happened?' he asked.

'I'll tell you in a minute,' Violet replied.

'How much trouble am I in?'

Art grimaced. 'Well, they did call the police.'

Everyone was sitting around the large table finishing lunch. Her mother and father got up as soon as they saw her.

'Violet, you are very naughty,' Benedict said sternly. Violet knew from experience that it was best to agree with whatever her parents said on these occasions.

'I know I am,' she replied, staring at the ground, looking sorry.

'Well, luckily for you,' Camille said. 'We have had two pieces of lovely news to distract us from your behaviour. The first is that Dee Dee's sister is feeling much better, so Dee

Dee is coming out here for the last week of the holiday. She arrives tonight on the late train. And the second, I will let Uncle Johnny tell you himself.'

Johnny was holding hands with Elena and looked delighted. 'Violet, I asked Elena to marry me this morning on the boat and she agreed.' He grinned.

First PC Green and now Uncle Johnny. What is happening to everyone? Violet wondered. She really liked Elena though, and

she could see that they were very happy.

'That's so nice. Congratulations.' She smiled and gave them both a hug.

'Isn't it marvellous?!' Grand-mère said. 'I do so approve of quick engagements. As your Grand-père used to say, when you know, you know. He asked me to marry him three hours after I met him!'

'PC Green's in love too,' Violet announced. 'With La Bellissima. He's guarding her while she's in Venice.' She was about to tell them that he was going to propose too, before she remembered it was supposed to be a secret.

'How sweet!' Grand-mère said.

'How unlikely,' Benedict added under his

breath, only to receive a stern look from Camille.

'I've just met her,' Violet said. 'And she invited us to the Opera tonight to watch her sing.'

Grand-mère's face lit up.

'Oh dear! Elena's parents have asked us all to dinner tonight to celebrate the engagement,' Camille said. 'And then we have to pick up Dee Dee from the station.'

Grand-mère's face fell.

Elena stepped in. 'I am sure my parents would understand if you went to see La Bellissima,' she said kindly to Grand-mère. 'It is an amazing opportunity.'

'Thank you, my dear,' Grand-mère replied, beaming.

'Violet, you had better go with Grand-mère, since La Bellissima invited you,' Camille said. 'But Art, I think you should come with us to meet Dee Dee. She'll be very keen to see you.'

Art nodded. He had really missed Dee Dee too.

'I agree but I think Rose will enjoy the Opera,' Grand-mère said. 'She is a very cultured little girl. Where is she, by the way?'

'I think she is in her bedroom,' Camille replied. 'She looked a bit upset earlier and didn't want any lunch. You haven't had a quarrel, have you?' she asked Violet.

Violet felt guilty remembering that she had been rather horrible to Rose.

'Maybe a little one,' Violet admitted.

'Well, you had better go and make it up,' Camille said firmly. 'Have you had lunch, *chérie?*'

Violet's stomach gave an angry growl in reply. 'Why don't you take the rest of this delicious pasta for you both to have upstairs? And look, there is yummy chocolate cake for pudding. Art, will you help Violet carry it all?'

Rose was lying on her bed reading, with Alphonse and the Maharani keeping her company. She said a loud hello to Art, but

ignored Violet. So Violet took a deep breath and did the right thing.

'I'm really sorry I was horrible to you. You are brave and much cleverer than me and I know I am not very sensible sometimes.'

'No, you're not,' replied Rose rather coldly.

'I should follow your advice more often,' Violet said.

'Yes, you should,' Rose said sniffily. But she sat up and started to eat the pasta Violet had brought her.

'So did you manage to follow Mr Jolly? Where did he go?' Art asked.

Violet was also munching away so answered between mouthfuls,

'He went into the Opera House with the boxes and never came out. I ran into PC Green and we searched the whole building but couldn't find anything. It doesn't make any sense.'

'That is strange,' Art said thoughtfully.

'Someone must be helping him inside the Opera House,' Rose said.

Violet nodded. 'PC Green thinks it's the manager.'

'Why?' asked Art.

'Because his eyes are too close together,'

Violet replied with a smile.

Art laughed and Rose allowed herself a small giggle.

'Also,' Violet explained to Rose 'I met La Bellissima and she invited us all to the Opera tonight. Art can't come because he is going to meet Dee Dee. Would you mind helping me try and intercept the smugglers then? I really need your help, please, Rose?' Violet asked her friend.

Rose paused for a moment, before saying, 'I suppose I could help you.'

'Oh, thank you, Rose,' Violet replied. 'And I promise to listen to you.'

'Okay, let's get to work,' Rose said. 'Time

for a crime-solving matrix. I think.'

'So, we still don't know who the Boss is,' Art said

'And we are not certain what they are smuggling, but we STRONGLY suspect that it is diamonds – remind me why?' Rose asked.

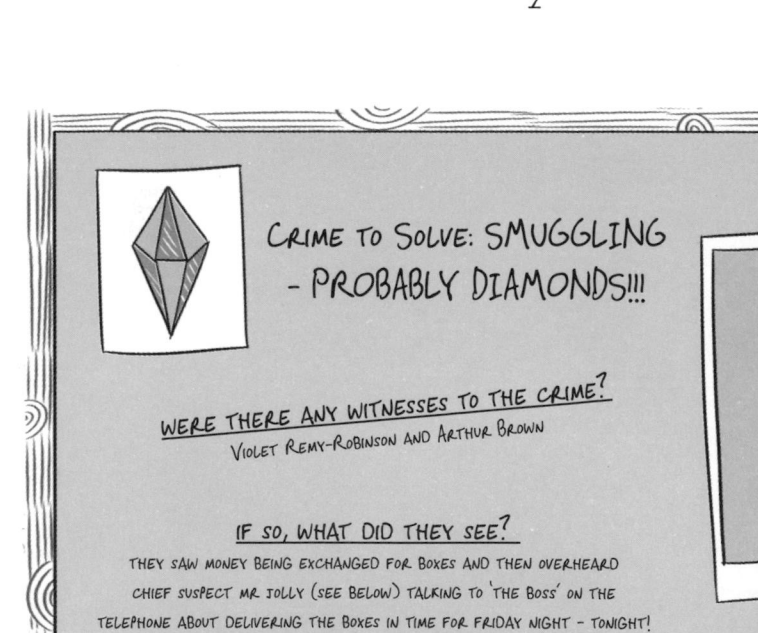

CRIME TO SOLVE: SMUGGLING
– PROBABLY DIAMONDS!!!

WERE THERE ANY WITNESSES TO THE CRIME?
VIOLET REMY-ROBINSON AND ARTHUR BROWN

IF SO, WHAT DID THEY SEE?
THEY SAW MONEY BEING EXCHANGED FOR BOXES AND THEN OVERHEARD
CHIEF SUSPECT MR JOLLY (SEE BELOW) TALKING TO 'THE BOSS' ON THE
TELEPHONE ABOUT DELIVERING THE BOXES IN TIME FOR FRIDAY NIGHT – TONIGHT!

'Because we know from the newspaper that there are diamond smugglers around and Art saw something sparkle in the box in Dubrovnik,' Violet replied.

'More gleam than sparkle,' Art said.

'Okay, and we think they are hidden in

WHAT CONCLUSIONS CAN BE DRAWN FROM THIS?
THAT THERE IS LIKELY TO BE A HANDOVER TONIGHT AT THE OPERA HOUSE

ARE THERE ANY SUSPECTS?
MR JOLLY AND 'THE BOSS' (IDENTITY UNKNOWN)

DO THEY HAVE A MOTIVE?
MONEY!!

DOES THIS LEAD YOU TO A SENSIBLE CONCLUSION?
WE NEED TO LOOK FOR MR JOLLY TONIGHT AT THE OPERA HOUSE, WHO WILL HOPEFULLY LEAD US TO 'THE BOSS' AND THE HANDOVER

something else because of the size of the boxes,' Rose said. 'We are pretty sure that something big happens tonight – the handover most likely – and we think it'll be at the Opera House. They'll have to do it somewhere out of sight, so we'll just take it in turns to go and look. We can pretend we need to go to the toilet, or get a drink of water, so that Grand-mère does not get suspicious.'

Violet thought for a moment, remembering all her cinema and theatre trips with Grand-mère over the years. 'I don't think we should worry too much, she always falls asleep,' Violet said.

At that moment the door flew open, revealing

Grand-mère, clutching her handbag.

'That is an outrageous suggestion, Violet. I do not! And I certainly won't while listening to La Bellissima. Now, I just came to tell you that I am off to the hairdresser and then I have decided to go shopping.'

Rose and Art nodded politely, vaguely wondering what that had to do with them, but Violet nearly shot off the bed in alarm.

'No, Grand-mère, please,' she cried, as

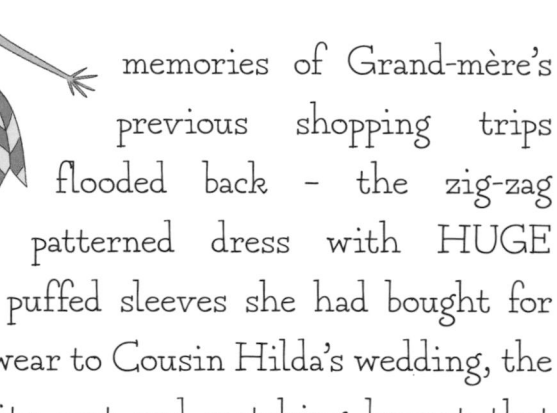

memories of Grand-mère's previous shopping trips flooded back - the zig-zag patterned dress with HUGE puffed sleeves she had bought for Violet to wear to Cousin Hilda's wedding, the furry white coat and matching bonnet that had made Violet look like a polar bear, the Heidi outfit from Austria with little shorts and braces. . .

'Really,' Violet went on. 'There is no need. I have a very smart dress already that I would love, love, love to wear. And Rose has a beautiful dress too.'

'Violet, do not deny an old woman her small

pleasures,' Grand-mère said firmly, and shut the door behind her.

Oh dear! Grand-mère's shopping trip was even worse than feared. Two hours later, Violet and Rose stood in front of Grand-mère and Signora Renaldo, who were both gazing delightedly at them.

'Don't they just look adorable?' Grand-mère exclaimed.

'*Perfecto*,' Signora Renaldo agreed. 'Like proper old-fashioned *bambini*.'

Benedict, Art and Johnny had left the room for fear of sniggering, but Camille and Elena remained, smiling sympathetically at the girls. And well they might be sympathetic, for Violet and Rose were dressed in very short white dresses with large, lace ruffles in tiers a bit like a Christmas tree and each lacy bit was edged with lilac bows. They wore white gloves and long lilac coloured socks with white shiny shoes, and Alphonse had a new bow tie to match. Just when they thought it couldn't get any worse, Grand-mère announced,

'Now I have arranged an extra-special treat to get us to the Opera House. The Singing Gondolier! It's going to be such fun!'

And so, Rose and Violet's embarrassment was complete as they travelled to the Opera House in a gondola with a gondolier singing at the top of his voice so that everyone stopped and stared at them, laughing and clapping.

Only Grand-mère looked delighted, grinning away with Alphonse on her lap, waving his paw at all the onlookers.

10
A HEART-SHAPED BOX OF CHOCOLATES

When they arrived at the Opera House, they were greeted by Luigi. He was very friendly and Rose agreed with Violet that whatever his eyes were like, he didn't seem very suspicious. He was even nice to Alphonse when the dog tried to bite him. He had nodded understandingly at Grand-mère when she'd apologised, saying that of course he was only a puppy. La Bellissima had arranged for them to sit in the royal box! None of them had ever been in a box before, let alone one as super-duper as that and Rose was particularly delighted. It was all gold and twirly inside, and instead of normal theatre seats, there were elegant chairs with velvet cushions. And, most importantly, it gave them a magnificent view of the auditorium. Luigi handed them a huge heart-shaped box of chocolates, saying,

'These are a very special gift from La Bellissima. You must try them, they are the most delicious chocolates in the whole world.'

Grand-mère tucked in as soon as Luigi had left, but Violet and Rose were still feeling a bit sick after the chocolate cake they had eaten earlier. And they were both rather nervous about finding the smugglers.

The lights dimmed and there was a hush as the orchestra began to play. The opera was *The Magic Flute* by the very famous composer, Mozart. La Bellissima was playing a scary lady called Queen of the Night and she soon appeared in an extraordinary costume and

heavy make-up, looking terrifying.

Rose was entirely swept away by the music and the beauty of it all, and found herself feeling a bit jealous of the girls in the chorus, who sang and danced around in pretty white dresses.

Violet, on the other hand, was certainly not swept away. Rarely had she been more bored and uncomfortable in her life. Her frilly dress was itching her and she was itching to go and search for Mr Jolly. She had scanned the outside of the Opera House as best she could from the gondola and had spent the few minutes they'd had in the box before the lights went down, peering around the auditorium. But there was no sign of Mr Jolly or anything else suspicious.

At last the music stopped and Violet, as they had planned earlier, got up and announced that she had to go to the loo.

'But, *chérie*, that is just the end of Act One. It is not the interval yet – can't you wait until then?' Grand-mère said to her.

'No, I'm desperate!' Violet replied.

'Okay, be quick,' she instructed as the music started up again.

But when Violet tried the door to the box it was locked. *How strange*, she thought. And then she thought, *How annoying!* How was she going to escape? Violet had seen

Art open doors with a piece of wire

wondered whether she could do it her

she had no wire with her. Violet

... ing she could use

... wait

but she

the box for someth...

There was nothing . . . unless, w...

eyes were drawn to Grand-mère's elaborate

hairstyle which involved lots of hairpins. One

of them might work, she decided, lunging at

the back of Grand-mère's head and pulling one

out quickly. Grand-mère twitched and patted

her hair but Violet got away with it. She

shoved the hairpin into the lock and jiggled

it around and, just when she thought she was

getting nowhere, the lock clicked and opened.

Violet slipped out of the door and set off. Of

she had no intention of going to the
was looking for Mr Jolly. And then,
to her amazement, she saw him
glimpse of his back

...m, or

...k and another man's
heading through a door marked
Privato. Violet was about to follow
them when she felt a hand on her
shoulder. She turned around to see
a very surprised looking Luigi.

'Is everything okay?' he asked.

'I was just going to the toilet.
Did you lock us in the box?' Violet
said.

'Yes, but La Bellissima told me it was what
you wanted,' Luigi replied. 'She said that you

were very scared about the smugglers.'

'No, I want to catch the smugglers! And I think I just saw one going through that door!'

'Really?' Luigi seemed genuinely amazed. 'Come, you are missing the Opera. I will escort you back to your box and then I will go and investigate.'

'Can't I come with you? Please?' Violet replied.

'No,' Luigi said firmly. 'Your grandmother will be worried and, besides, catching smugglers is not a matter for little girls.' And reluctantly, Violet followed him. Sometimes it was impossible to argue with grown-ups.

Back in the box, Grand-mère was fast asleep.

Rose helped herself to one of La Bellissima's chocolates as Violet whispered to her all that had happened.

'Why would La Bellissima say that?' Rose asked, puzzled.

'I don't know, but we really need to go and investigate now!'

Rose hesitated. 'Maybe we should wait for the interval?' she said. 'Otherwise, won't we just run into Luigi and then he might be cross and lock us in again?'

Violet was about to disagree but she remembered her promise to listen to Rose. And it couldn't be more than twenty minutes until the interval, she decided, so she nodded and tried to concentrate on the Opera.

Quite a long twenty minutes later, the music finally stopped, the curtain came down and the lights went up for the interval. Grand-mère was still fast asleep, snoring contentedly with Alphonse at her feet. Rose was feeling a little sleepy herself as Violet grabbed her by the hand and galloped off in search of Mr Jolly.

The door marked *Privato* led up a staircase to a door with a large gold star on it.

'This must be La Bellissima's dressing room,' Rose said. 'Do you think—' she began, but Violet was already knocking briskly. When she didn't get an immediate response, she turned the handle, opening the door to reveal PC Green, down on one knee before La Bellissima. She wasn't looking at him. She was holding a ring up to the light, examining it carefully.

'Girls!' PC Green protested when he saw them. 'Violet, I told you, this is my big moment!'

'I'm really, really sorry, I totally forgot,' she said, which was actually true. There were more important things to worry about! 'I saw Mr Jolly come up here during the performance.'

A look of irritation passed across La Bellissima's face that she quickly replaced with one of alarm, but not before the girls had noticed it.

'No! The smugglers came up here!' she exclaimed. 'Perhaps they are on the roof,' she said fearfully. 'Reginald, would you check for me? And thank you so much for your kind offer of marriage. Would you mind waiting just a few days before I give you my answer? It is such a huge decision to make.' Rose noticed she slipped the ring, which presumably PC Green has just given to her, into her pocket.

'Of course, my love,' he beamed. 'Take as long as you need. Just make sure you say yes in the end!' he added, with a playful wag of his finger, and he set off down the corridor.

'Now, girls, are you enjoying the performance? I hope you liked the chocolates?' La Bellissima asked innocently.

'Oh, yes!' Rose replied, smothering a yawn. 'I just had some. They were delicious.'

'Good. And you, Violet?'

Violet didn't want to offend her. 'Me too. They were yummy,' she said politely.

'Excellent,' La Bellissima replied. There was yet another knock on the door and a stage hand put her head around.

'Two minutes, Boss.'

Violet gave a start at the mention of 'Boss'. La Bellissima noticed and tried to make a joke of it. 'That's what everyone calls me, because I can be a little bossy!' she said with a forced smile. 'Now, girls, I must go, I'm needed on stage. You wait for Reginald in here. I am sure he will be back in a moment. Ciao.' And she swept out of the room before the girls could say anything else.

'That stage hand just called her "Boss"!' Violet cried, when she was gone, her brain ticking away. 'That's what Mr Jolly called the person on the phone! Rose, what if La Bellissima is the boss of the smugglers?'

'Well, that would explain the boxes being delivered here. And it would also explain why she would want to lock us in our box,' Rose said.

'Yes, and she started the trend for DIAMOND encrusted tortoises,' Violet cried. 'And she is leaving for Amsterdam tonight; that's where the newspaper said the diamonds were being smuggled to!'

'We must tell PC Green,' Rose said.

Violet gasped. 'Do you think that is why she is being so nice to him? To stop him suspecting anything?'

'Maybe,' Rose replied. 'Perhaps we shouldn't tell him that, though. He'll be awfully upset.'

'But he might want to get his ring back,' Violet pointed out.

'He might, but I think we should have more proof first,' Rose said, going to open the door. She turned the handle both ways. It wouldn't budge.

'What's the matter?' Violet asked.

'It's locked,' Rose replied. 'La Bellissima's locked us in.'

11
TARATUGAS AND TRUNKS

'PC Green, PC Green!' Rose and Violet shouted, banging on the door as loudly as they could. But no one came.

What they didn't know was that, after she had locked them in, La Bellissima had bumped straight into PC Green, who was returning from the roof, just as she had hoped.

'The girls have gone back to their seats,' she lied. 'Please, I am so scared, will you walk me to the stage, Reginald darling?'

PC Green glowed with pride and love. 'My

pleasure,' he replied, offering her his arm.

Violet looked around the room for another means of escape. There was a window, but beneath it was a sheer drop to the Square below. Violet was an excellent climber, and even she couldn't manage a climb like that.

'Look! There's another door,' Rose said, between yawns. 'Hidden behind that screen.'

'Yes, and it's open!' Violet said, rushing over and trying the door handle. 'Rose, you are so clever.

But the door didn't lead into the corridor as the girls had hoped, but instead into another small dressing room that was full of rails of costumes, three trunks and a pile of suitcases.

'It's just her luggage,' Rose said, plonking herself down on one of the trunks.

There was another window, which instead of opening onto the Square, looked out onto the back of the stage. *Not much use*, Violet thought but was then distracted by spotting Mr Jolly's boxes piled in a corner of the room.

'Ah ha!' she cried, excited again. But again she was disappointed because they were empty. *If they are empty*, Violet thought, *that means that whatever Mr Jolly kept in the boxes is*

somewhere in this room. Her thoughts were interrupted by Rose leaping off the trunk as if something had bitten her.

'That trunk is moving!' Rose screeched.

Violet put one hand gingerly on the trunk and pulled it back very fast as she realised Rose was right.

'What do you think is in there?' Rose asked tremulously. 'A person?'

Had La Bellissima taken someone captive?

'Hello,' Violet said nervously. 'Can you hear me? Do you speak English?'

'Maybe they're gagged and can't answer?' Rose suggested. 'Look, there are air holes you can look through.'

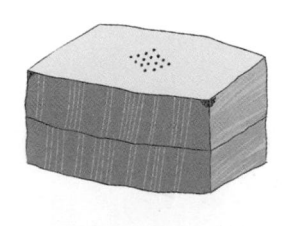

Violet tentatively put her eye up to one.

'It's too dark in there – I can't see anything,' she announced. 'We have to open it.'

'No!' Rose looked terrified at the thought. Then, trying to be a bit braver, she added, 'Maybe it won't even open?'

Violet (who was half-wishing Rose was right) tried the latch. It sprung open. She turned her face away in case there was something really horrid in there and slowly lifted the lid . . . and then she gasped.

'I don't believe it,' she said. 'Rose, you have to come and see what's in here.'

'Is it something scary?' Rose asked nervously.

'Not scary at all, just very strange. Come and look,' Violet urged her.

Rose approached the trunk and peered in nervously, 'That's so odd,' she said. 'Why would La Bellissima have all these tortoises? There must be about twenty of them here.'

'Look!' Violet cried, opening the other two trunks. 'There are more in these!'

Both girls were silent again, thinking.

'Rose, I think I've been wrong all along,'

Violet said. 'It's not diamonds they're smuggling – it's tortoises!'

Before Rose could reply, the sound of heavy footsteps and voices came from down the corridor.

'Quick. Hide,' Violet whispered, diving behind a clothes rail. Rose stood frozen with fear for a moment, then, as the door opened, in a panic and unable to see anywhere else to hide, she opened the lid of one of the trunks and carefully crouched between the tortoises. She shut the trunk lid above her head.

Through a gap in the clothes, Violet saw Mr Jolly appear with the man who had been with him earlier. They were talking quickly in Italian.

'We had better watch out for those pesky English children,' Mr Jolly said.

'They won't be bothering us. The Boss dealt with them – she gave them a huge box of chocolates with sleeping pills in them. They'll be snoring away happily, and by the time they wake up, we'll be gone.'

Violet gasped. No wonder Grand-mère had been asleep. But what about Rose? She had eaten some chocolates before the interval and she had been yawning . . .

'Right, let's shift these trunks onto that fool's police boat. The Boss will be coming off stage in fifteen minutes and then it's straight

to the railway station for the eleven - twenty train to Amsterdam where these little beauties will get their diamond coats.'

'Doesn't the Boss ever worry she might get searched by customs?'

'That idiot of a policeman would never allow his beloved to be searched, and besides, who is ever going to suspect a big star like La Bellissima of being a smuggler?'

Violet's eyes widened as they picked up the trunk with Rose inside.

'Oof! These tortoises have been eating too much cabbage!' Mr Jolly complained, and Violet watched in horror as they carried the trunk out of the room.

Please leave the door open! Violet thought, but then a moment later she heard the key turn in the lock. Violet tried not to panic. She had to get out of this room and rescue Rose before she fell asleep in the trunk and woke up to find herself in Amsterdam. And what about all the tortoises? *Think!* Violet instructed herself. There were only ten minutes at most until Mr Jolly and his friend came back so she had to get out of there and find help. She looked around the dressing room again – both doors were locked, one window had a sheer drop onto the Square and the other . . . the other looked out on the back of the stage. Without any other options, Violet went over to the stage window.

I don't know if you have ever seen backstage at an Opera House, but behind the neat scenery is a complicated jumble of layers of more scenery, metal bars with lights attached – which are called rigs – and ropes and pulleys to move everything.

So when Violet opened the window, that was the sight that greeted her, along with a long drop down to the stage. And unfortunately, even with Violet's climbing experience, there wasn't a rope close enough to help her get from the window to the stage easily. Trying not to panic, she worked out a route with her eyes that involved jumping onto one rope and then another, walking along two lighting rigs, before she could reach a rope long enough to make her escape. She took a deep breath, climbed out onto the window sill and began.

12
A STAR IS BORN

Violet carefully gripped the first rope, jumped gracefully to the second and then lowered herself onto a rig. The metal was slippery and swung alarmingly from side to side, but luckily there was a rope running alongside that she used to steady herself as she teetered along.

Now, when Violet was nervous she talked to herself, and the voice that answered her back wasn't always that helpful, as you will see now.

Come on, she told herself strictly. *Think of all the climbing you have done. This is just the same.*

Is it? replied unhelpful Violet. *But you were always wearing a harness so it didn't matter if you fell.*

But I didn't ever fall.

What about the time you fell out of the tree . . . ?

Oh, be quiet! she said and, gripping the rope with all her strength, she pushed off and swung to the other rig. She touched lightly down on it, with a ballet-dancer-like gracefulness that she knew would have made Rose proud. But this time there wasn't another rope to hold on to, so poor Violet had to inch along the rig on all fours. This would have been bad enough, but the whole thing was shaking as if it were about to collapse under her weight. Violet was truly scared now and despite trying her best not to look down, she kept catching glimpses of the stage a very long way below.

The unhelpful voice in her head returned with a vengeance.

You think it hurt when you fell out of that tree, just wait until you fall from here. You are going to be squished on the stage and probably die . . .

Shush! she said, as her heart thumped in her chest. Miraculously, when she had almost given up hope, she found the rope she had been aiming for was just in front of her. With a small sigh of relief, she pulled herself onto the rope. Now all she had to do was climb down it, which for most people would be very, very difficult if not impossible. You can't let yourself go too fast, otherwise you get terrible rope burns. You have to come down slowly, hand over hand, and that takes a lot of effort. Luckily Violet was exceptionally good at these things, but unfortunately she had only gone a short way when something very annoying happened.

It suddenly became very dark and then the stage beneath her, which had been empty, was flooded with people dressed in black who began moving things around, getting ready for the final scene of the Opera. Violet's hands and arms were aching so much that she was desperate to get off the rope, but she couldn't risk one of the people below seeing her. She was trying to decide what to do when there was a roar of applause from the audience and, alarmingly, the scenery started to move around her. Then one of the stage hands looked up.

'What are you doing?' he whispered fiercely in Italian. 'Come down this instant. You are meant to be waiting in the wings to go on, not messing around back here. It's very dangerous.'

He must think I'm in the Opera, Violet thought, as she climbed quickly down the rest of the rope, wondering why he would believe such a thing.

When she reached the ground she saw a gaggle of children waiting at the side of the stage. *Of course*, she thought, remembering watching them in the first half, *they are all dressed in white like me*. That was why the man had thought she was part of the show. She desperately tried to think of a way to escape, but the man was hovering nearby, so she walked to the back of the group. They eyed her suspiciously.

'Are you new?' a boy asked her in Italian.

Violet nodded, looking back into the wings to see if she could escape, but the way was blocked by a crowd of other performers.

'Why weren't you in any of the rehearsals?' a girl asked bossily.

Violet shrugged. She was just about to turn and try to push her way through, when to her horror, she saw La Bellissima approaching.

'On stage now, everyone!' she instructed, and the children all obediently scuttled ahead of her to take their places before the lights came up again. Violet knew that if she didn't go with them, La Bellissima would notice her immediately, so with no other choice, she walked out onto the darkened stage.

Violet went right to the far side of the stage, intending to walk off the other side, when she felt an icy grip on her arm.

'What are *you* doing here?' La Bellissima hissed, her face a terrifying mask of make-up and fury, all pretence at niceness gone. 'How did you get out of my dressing room? You and your friend are such annoying little brats!'

At that moment the lights went on and La Bellissima let go of Violet as she span away and began to sing, leaving Violet frozen and blinking at the sea of faces that had suddenly appeared.

Unlike Rose, Violet did not enjoy being on stage. The few school shows she'd had to take part in had been awful and this was much worse, because she had no idea what she was supposed to do. She tried to mouth as if she were singing and copy what the other children were doing, but she kept bumping into them, as they shot her furious looks.

The children weren't the only people who were angry. La Bellissima was so annoyed that she was struggling to focus on her singing. She could see Violet blundering around the stage

from the corner of her eye, and she could hear titters of laughter coming from the audience. Not only was this wretched child trying to ruin her smuggling plans, she was now spoiling her last night's performance in Venice. La Bellissima longed to grab her by the ear and drag her off the stage, but she realised that would only make her look mean. Where was that useless manager or hopeless policeman when she needed them?

The singing was reaching a crescendo and Violet decided it was now or never. She knew that if she went backstage, Luigi or one of the stage hands would stop her, so she made a bold decision. She ran down one of the sets of side stairs that led off the stage into the auditorium and up the main central aisle towards the green-lighted sign, which read 'EXIT'. The audience thought she was hilarious and clapped and cheered her as the final scene ended. Violet burst through a set of double doors into the foyer and dashed through the main entrance doors, desperate to find Rose and the poor tortoises. She whirled around, trying to spot any clues as to where they might have gone, but there was no sign of them at the front in the square, or at the stage door. Where had they disappeared to?

With the Opera over, people were beginning

to pour out of the building, and Violet had a brainwave. The water gate, where they had been dropped earlier by the Singing Gondolier! She dashed around the side of Opera House and there, at the end of a narrow jetty, was the police boat, laden with luggage. PC Green stood at the steering wheel. Violet bounded towards the boat. She'd found them before they'd left!

At that moment La Bellissima swept out onto the jetty and into the boat, still dressed as Queen of the Night.

'Drive!' she commanded PC Green. 'I will

miss my train otherwise.'

PC Green started the engine.

'No!' shouted Violet, running up to them. 'You can't go. PC Green! Rose is in one of those trunks, as well as loads of tortoises!'

'I can hardly hear you over the engine, Violet. What did you say?' PC Green shouted.

'She said nothing of any importance, Reginald. I will be late! Go!' La Bellissima shrieked at PC Green.

'Sorry, Violet,' he yelled back. 'We've got a train to catch. I guess you didn't find your smuggler but you can tell me about it

tomorrow. Let's have an ice cream. *Ciao ciao.*'

'She's the main smuggler!' Violet shouted as loudly as she could.

PC Green was too busy revving the boat's engine to hear, but La Bellissima did, and she turned to Violet, stamping her foot angrily.

'Someone needs to shut you up once and for all! A silly child like you won't get in my way!' she hissed and, leaning over, gave Violet an almighty shove, sending her head-first into the canal as the boat sped off.

13
ARRIVEDERCI?

Falling into the canal was not a pleasant experience for poor Violet. The only good thing was that the water wasn't cold. Instead it was lukewarm, murky, a bit smelly and generally disgusting, so when Violet scrambled out onto the jetty, she was feeling extremely sorry for herself, as well as terribly worried for Rose and the tortoises. Sopping wet, she squelched back to the front of the Opera House and spotted Grand-mère and Alphonse. Grand-mère was shouting at Luigi.

'You are telling me that you have lost my granddaughter and her friend. I demand that you call the police!'

'*Ruff ruff ruff ruff,*' Alphonse joined in.

'Gladly, *Signora*. If you will just wait here . . .' Luigi agreed, happy to have a chance to escape.

'Violet! Thank goodness!' Grand-mère exclaimed when she saw her. 'Why are you all wet? I woke up to see you on the stage. What were you doing there? And where is Rose?'

'La Bellissima pushed me into the canal! She's a tortoise smuggler and Rose is in one of La Bellissima's trunks on her way to the

WOOF!!
WOOF!!

station to be put on a train to Amsterdam.'

Grand-mère looked extremely alarmed. 'Mon dieu! What a lot of terrible information in one sentence. It sounds as if we must get to the station to rescue Rose.'

There were rows of moored boats and water taxis, picking people up from the Opera. Grand-mère and Violet ran up and down asking if they were free but they were all taken.

'It's hopeless. The train will be gone in ten minutes,' Violet said, thinking that she might cry.

'We are going to have to steal, I mean, borrow, a boat,' Grand-mère announced in a matter of fact way. 'Look for a boat with keys

in, Violet.'

'Here's one,' Grand-mère announced a few seconds later, climbing nimbly down into an empty speed boat, Alphonse tucked under one arm. 'Do not fret over the time. As you know, I am a very fast driver.'

Violet jumped in after her and held on for dear life as Grand-mère sped off.

'Will you find my glasses for me, chérie?' Grand-mère asked, thrusting her handbag at Violet, as she slammed through some buoys.

There was some loud shouting as they narrowly missed a boat coming towards them.

'Honestly, people make such a fuss. Can't they see we are in a hurry?! How are we doing for time?'

Violet looked at her watch. 'Five minutes until the train leaves!'

'I had better put my foot down then. Forget about my glasses.'

Violet shut her eyes while poor Alphonse was huddled in the bottom of the boat.

And then with a final flourish, Grand-mère swung the boat sharply to one side, coming to a very abrupt halt and sending up a large plume of water, soaking them all.

'*Voila*! The station – and all without my glasses on.'

As it was late at night, the station was quiet. Violet ran ahead of Grand-mère to scan the departures board for the Amsterdam train. It was on platform five, leaving in two minutes. She sprinted off and nearly bumped straight into Benedict, Camille, Art and Dee Dee, who had just arrived on the London train together with an array of matching suitcases.

'Violet, my darling! What a lovely surprise! And what a charming outfit!' Dee Dee cried, when she saw her.

'Hello, what are you doing here?' Benedict asked, looking confused.

'I can't stop,' Violet panted. 'Rose is in a trunk full of tortoises on the train to Amsterdam, which leaves in two minutes. She's with La Bellissima – who's a tortoise smuggler! Come on, Art!' And they ran off towards platform five, leaving the others looking astonished.

'I think we had better go and see what is going on,' Camille said calmly.

When La Bellissima travelled she occupied a whole first class compartment. As Violet and Art neared the platform, they could see PC Green clutching the opera singer's hand as she leaned out of the train window, looking

intensely bored.

But between the children and the train were Mr Jolly and his accomplice. Art and Violet tried to dodge the men, but they were too quick and grabbed them. The station guard who was at the other end of the platform, blew his whistle. 'All aboard!' he shouted in Italian.

'PC Green!' Violet shouted desperately. 'You have to stop the train. La Bellissima has Rose and loads of tortoises in her luggage! She's going to smuggle them to Amsterdam and fill their shells full of diamonds, and goodness

knows what she'll do with Rose' — Mr Jolly clamped his hand over her mouth.

PC Green turned to La Bellissima enquiringly, who suddenly didn't look bored at all. She grabbed PC Green by his shirt collars, saying,

'I say yes to your proposal. Kiss me, Reginald!' And before he had a chance to speak, she pulled him towards her.

Meanwhile, Violet and Art were struggling like captured tigers with the men. The station guard appeared from the other end of the platform looking concerned.

'GET YOUR HANDS OFF THOSE CHILDREN!!' Benedict yelled, sprinting towards them. Startled, the two men did as they were told, scared now that they were faced with a very angry-looking Benedict, and quickly ran off. But it was too late. The train had started to move off, slowly but surely.

PC Green was left on the platform looking lovingly after La Bellissima, who smiled smugly as she called out: '*Arrivederci*, Reginald! *Arrivederci*, Violet!'

'NO!' Violet cried and burst into hot, angry tears.

'There goes my love,' PC Green sighed. 'Now what was going on with those men over there, Violet?'

Grand-mère arrived at that moment, along

with Dee Dee and Camille.

'Where is Rose?' Grand-mère cried. 'Do not tell me,' she said, poking PC Green with her finger, 'that you did not listen to my grand-daughter and you have let that tortoise smuggler escape? And with Rose on board!' Alphonse had a jolly good bark at him too.

'That is my beloved you are talking about,' PC Green said stoutly. 'We are to be married after her tour.'

'Oh, don't be ridiculous,' Grand-mère said. 'She has played you for the fool you clearly are. Guard, stop that train!'

'Bit harsh, Madam,' PC Green said, wounded.

Meanwhile the guard said, 'Signora, I cannot.

The train, it is already gone.'

'Where is the next stop?' Camille asked.

'Munich,' the guard replied.

'MUNICH!' everyone cried. 'But that's in Germany!'

'Is my precious Rose really on that train?' Dee Dee said looking alarmed. 'I cannot bear it! Something must be done!'

And everyone started shouting, rather unfairly, at the poor guard.

14
JUST A FEW LITTLE PETS . . .

Meanwhile, on the train, Rose was very much awake. The sleeping pills had taken effect almost as soon as she'd hidden in the trunk, but all the pushing and shoving that Mr Jolly and his friend had done to get the trunk onto the train had woken her up.

Now, imagine lying squashed up in a very dark place surrounded by a lot of tortoises. However much you like tortoises, it's not going to be very nice. So, naturally, Rose was very keen to get out of the trunk as soon as possible. And when she found the lid of the trunk locked, she started banging on it. But no one came. And then she felt wherever she was start to move, which caused poor Rose to really panic and bang even harder.

A few seconds later, the lid opened to reveal La Bellissima, still in her scary make-up and costume, staring down at her.

'Oh, so you are in there. How annoying!' La Bellissima rolled her eyes. 'Now climb out in case you damage my precious tortoises. You can sleep in a corner and then you'll have to get off the train at Munich in the morning.' She pulled Rose up by her collar with surprising strength

and lifted her out of the trunk. Rose looked around. She hadn't realised they were on a train until that moment and she could see the last bit of the platform disappearing from view.

'Munich?' stammered Rose. 'But I haven't got any money or a passport. I don't know anyone in Munich. . .' Rose could feel the panic rising in her stomach and tears beginning to fill her eyes.

'You should have thought of that before you started poking your nose into my business and hiding in my trunk. Now I am very tired after my concert, so stop that annoying noise and just be quiet.' And La Bellissima settled herself down on a seat with her back to Rose. She opened her vanity case and proceeded to cover her face in thick cream to take off her make-up.

The train was gaining speed and Rose wiped away her tears impatiently. There must be something she could do. *What would Violet do?* she asked herself. All hope seemed lost when suddenly she saw it, like a little red beacon floating above the seats: the emergency brake. Grand-mère's words came floating back: *Sometimes in life, if you are going somewhere you don't want to go, you have to be brave and pull the emergency brake.*

Rose was in no doubt that this was just such

a time. She launched herself across the carriage towards the lever, clambering up on a seat to reach it. There was a colossal screeching of brakes as the train heaved and juddered to a halt. La Bellissima span around, her face a mess of cream and smeared make-up, one false eye lash dangling down her cheek like a spider. When she saw Rose hanging onto the brake lever, she lunged at her.

The carriage door shot open and in came a guard. She was a young, friendly-looking woman with a very concerned expression on her face.

'What has happened? Why did you pull the brake?' she asked Rose in Italian.

Rose's mouth was dry with fear but she managed to say in a whisper, 'Do you speak English?'

'I do,' she replied in perfect English. 'It was my favourite subject at school.'

'Oh, good,' Rose began. 'Well, you see—'

'This child is a criminal and a stowaway,' La Bellissima interrupted furiously. 'I found her in my trunk.'

The guard gave La Bellissima a surprised look. 'You found a stowaway child in your trunk and you weren't going to report it? Do you know her? Why do you think she is a criminal?'

'Of course I was going to report it. . .at some point. Do you know who I am?'

'At this moment I am more interested in hearing what this young girl is doing on the train alone.'

La Bellissima drew herself up, a little like a rattle snake does before it strikes.

'I am La Bellissima, the world famous Opera Star, and this child is some little nosy nobody. Now, do you have a man in charge of you that I could talk to?'

The guard was silent for a moment. Rose could see she was struggling not to say something really rude to La Bellissima.

'No, I don't, Madam. I could take you to see the train driver, but she, too, is a woman,' she said and then turned back to Rose. 'Now where is your family?'

'In London,' Rose replied, and then added quickly. 'But I have been staying with friends in Venice.'

'Are they still there?'

Rose nodded and the guard began to speak into her radio, saying something to the driver in Dutch that Rose didn't understand. A moment later the train started reversing back into Venice station.

'Wonderful! Thank you!' La Bellissima replied, smiling prettily at the guard. 'Now at least I won't have to put up with a snivelling brat all the way to Munich. Are we done now?'

'And why were you in the trunk?' the guard asked Rose, still ignoring La Bellissima.

'Because of the tortoises,' Rose replied.

'The tortoises?' The guard sounded baffled. 'Show me, please.'

La Bellissima began to object loudly but the guard ignored her and examined all three trunks silently. Then she turned and asked La Bellissima very politely,

'Madam, please can you show me the documentation for exporting these tortoises?'

Back on the station platform everyone was still very cross with the guard. And they were so busy being cross that it was only Art who noticed something.

'Shush, everyone!' he cried. 'The train has stopped!'

They all fell silent and peered down the track.

'You are right, young man,' the guard said. 'That means there is either a problem with the train or someone has pulled the emergency brake.'

Grand-mère let out a gasp of excitement. 'It will be Rose, I am sure of it! She is such a sensible child. She must have found she was on a train she did not want to be on, so she pulled the emergency brake, just as I taught her. Just watch, the train will reverse in a minute.'

They all stared at the stationary train, and then the guard's radio crackled and a voice started babbling in Italian.

'You are right, Madam,' he announced, when the voice had stopped, 'the little girl pulled the brake and they will reverse the train to bring her back.'

Everyone cheered.

'And,' the guard said to PC Green, 'they are asking for the police to be here, as there is a criminal aboard.'

PC Green gasped. 'A criminal! Do you think my love is in any danger?'

'La Bellissima is the criminal!' Violet said. 'That's what we've been trying to tell you—'

'Oh, don't be silly, Violet,' PC Green interrupted. 'How could someone that pretty be a crook? It's simply not possible. I'd better call for reinforcements in case I need a hand.' And he got busy on his radio.

It just so happened that the Chief of Police was finishing a late dinner nearby. After hearing the radio message, he decided he would go and see the English policeman in action for himself.

He arrived as the train was pulling in.

The train door opened and out jumped Rose,

looking extremely relieved, followed by the guard, and lastly, La Bellissima. She seemed to have forgotten that she had only got halfway through taking off her make-up so was looking a little strange. Violet and everyone else grouped around Rose, while the Chief of Police marched up to PC Green.

'Green, where is the criminal?'

The train guard answered for him. 'This is her. This lady has about sixty tortoises in her luggage and no paperwork.'

PC Green looked shocked. 'Is it really true, my love?' he asked.

'I had no idea I was not allowed a few little pets,' La Bellissima protested.

'Sixty pets?' the Chief of Police asked.

'I cannot help it if I am an animal lover,' she said, pouting.

'No, but you can help being a smuggler,' he replied.

'A smuggler?' La Bellissima gasped in horror. 'How dare you? Reginald, will you not defend my honour?'

'Er, yes, Sir, I am sure this isn't a deliberate act of smuggling. It's just a mistake. . .'

The Chief of Police raised his eyebrows. 'Well, let us sort out this "mistake" at the police station. Madam, you will have to come with me now.'

'I will not! Reginald, sort this out!' she

shrieked at PC Green.

'Um, well, I'm not sure I can, my love. The evidence seems to be there and it is a crime so. . .'

La Bellissima let out a bellow of frustration.

'Oh, shut up, you fool! And don't call me "my love"! I'm not your love – as if I ever would be! You are a boring, annoying, useless little man!' she snarled at him.

PC Green looked as if he might cry. Then to everyone's delight, he blinked back his tears and said in a dignified way,

'Madam, you are not the woman I thought you were. I withdraw my offer of marriage and ask that you kindly return my great-grandmother's engagement ring.'

'With pleasure! Such a teeny little diamond I could hardly see it!' La Bellissima spat back, fishing the ring out of her pocket and flinging it at PC Green.

'Come on, Madam,' the Chief of

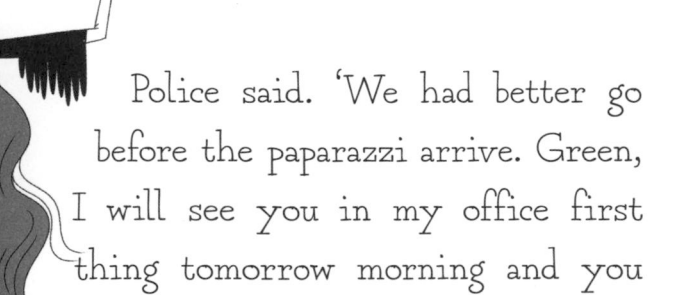

Police said. 'We had better go before the paparazzi arrive. Green, I will see you in my office first thing tomorrow morning and you can explain why you failed to notice that the woman you have spent the last week with is a tortoise smuggler.'

'Goodness me, what an eventful evening!' Grand-mère said, as they walked back through the station. La Bellissima had been dragged off by the Chief of Police and they had waved goodbye to the nice guard as the train left for the second time for Amsterdam. They had apologised to the station guard for all the shouting and everyone was just debating whether they should walk home or take a taxi boat when Violet noticed that PC Green was sitting forlornly on a nearby bench. She went over to him, followed by Rose and Art.

'PC Green?' she said.

'Not for much longer, I shouldn't think,' he said, with a heavy sigh. 'I'm bound to lose my job over this. I wonder whether they'll let me keep the uniform at least,' he said sadly, looking down at his lovely shiny boots.

'I'm sure they will,' Rose said comfortingly.

'I'm sorry I didn't believe you, chaps.' He paused and rubbed his eyes.

'She called me a fool and I am a fool. I really thought she loved me,' he said. The children all nodded sympathetically, feeling a little awkward.

'How about an ice cream?' Art suggested.

PC Green looked up, a little like a lost dog whose owner has just called its name.

'I suppose I might be able to force one down,' he said, standing up. 'And there is that great all night place near here.' He got to his feet. 'They do the best fudgey-caramel flavour you have ever tasted, honestly, chaps, it is to die for. Come on, where's everyone else? You have to get them to come too . . .'

And they all linked arms and set off into the warm summer night.

ENGLISH CHILD DETECTIVES BUST
TORTOISE SMUGGLING RING
Beauty AND THE BEASTS -
ITALIAN OPERA SINGER LA BELLISSIMA EXPOSED
AS TORTOISE SMUGGLER!

THE TORTOISE AND THE STAR! ARRESTED
- LA BELLISSIMA CAUGHT WITH NEARLY <u>60</u> TORTOISES!

NOT SO BELLISSIMA NOW! <u>UGLY</u> SIDE OF WORLD'S
MOST *beautiful* OPERA SINGER

THE FONTANA TORTOISE SANCTUARY,
LUCCA,
ITALY

5TH SEPTEMBER

Dear Violet, Rose and Art,

I just wanted to write to let you know that the tortoises you rescued have arrived safe and sound, delivered by your enchanting friend PC GREEN. We have over five kilometres of gardens for them to play in so I am sure they will have a happy life! Please feel free to visit at any time and please pass on my warmest regards to Reginald.

Yours Sincerely,

Maria Fontana

ANNOUNCEMENTS

VENICE TIMES, 2ND SEPTEMBER

THIS SATURDAY SEES A DOUBLE CELEBRATION AT THE PENSIONE RENALDO.
THE FIRST HAPPY OCCASION IS THE PRESENTATION IN THE MORNING AT THE PALAZZO RIGA
OF THE ANCIENT ORDER OF THE TORTOISE TO THE THREE ENGLISH CHILDREN, ROSE, VIOLET AND
ARTHUR, WHO UNCOVERED THE TORTOISE SMUGGLING RING, SUPPOSEDLY HEADED BY OPERA
SUPERSTAR, LA BELLISSIMA. THE PRESTIGIOUS ORDER IS AWARDED TO ANYONE WHO PERFORMS
EXCEPTIONAL SERVICES TO TORTOISES.

THE SECOND DELIGHTFUL REASON FOR CELEBRATION IS THE WEDDING AT THE
PENSIONE RENALDO OF MR JOHNNY BAXTER AND MISS ELENA RENALDO. THE HAPPY
COUPLE WILL BE HONEYMOONING ON MR BAXTER'S BOAT, THE APTLY NAMED,
IL TARATUGA.

After

This book started with a letter and ends with a speech.

Ting! Ting! Johnny hit his glass with the side of his knife for silence as he stood up, looking very dashing in a grey suit. The hotel courtyard was lit prettily with fairy lights and candles, and crammed full of long trestle tables piled high with flowers and food. Around the tables sat a lot of happy people.

'Ladies and Gentlemen! *Signore e Signori!*' Johnny began. 'Thank you so much for coming to our wedding!' Everyone cheered. 'I know it was a very brief engagement but as Grand-mère says, when you know, you know.'

'Here! Here!' PC Green cried. He was sitting holding hands with Maria, the lady from the tortoise sanctuary. He had brought her as his date to the wedding. She smiled shyly at him, blushing.

'I would, of course, like to start by thanking Elena for doing me the great honour of becoming my wife. I am an incredibly lucky man.' There were lots of cheers and applause as Johnny bent to kiss his bride.

On the other side of the table, Dee Dee whispered to her new best friend, Grand-mère, 'Weddings always make me cry.'

'Me too,' Grand-mère agreed and they

both mopped their eyes with matching lace handkerchiefs.

'Now,' Johnny went on. 'I also want to thank my fantastic best men, Benedict and Art, and the marvellous bridesmaids, Rose and Violet, who look so lovely in their dresses.' At this Johnny winked at the girls. Dee Dee and Grand-mère had tried to join forces to argue for 'proper' bridesmaid dresses – which meant lacy, puffy, froufrou nightmares. Luckily, Camille and Elena had held firm with Violet and Rose for something simpler. So the girls now sat in pretty, pale blue sundresses with just a few flowers pinned into their hair.

'Elena and I can't wait to set sail for

our honeymoon, travelling around the Mediterranean. After such an exciting summer, I'm sure it will be another great adventure. So, please can everyone raise your glasses and join with me in a toast to adventures. May your lives always be full of them!'

Everyone stood and raised their glasses. 'To adventures!' they all cried, even Rose.

Violet's extra-helpful word glossary

Violet loves words, especially if they sound unusual, so some of the words used in her story might have been a little tricky to understand. Most of them you probably know, but Violet has picked out a few to explain . . .

Astronomical – Means very high.

Buona Sera – Means 'good evening' in Italian

Constellations – These are collections of stars and the Big Dipper is a famous one.

Sceptical – This means if you are not sure something is true.

The French Resistance – This was a group of very brave people in the Second World War who fought against the Nazi Occupation of France. There is lots of information online about it, if you want to know more.

Zuppa Inglese – Trifle-flavoured ice cream

Frutti Di Bosca – Wild strawberry-flavoured ice cream.

Stracciatella – Vanilla-flavoured ice cream with chocolate flakes.

Pistachio – Nutty-flavoured ice cream.

Bambini – Means 'children' in Italian.

Brava – Means 'good' in Italian and Bravissimo means "very good".

LOOK OUT FOR
VIOLET AND THE PEARL
OF THE ORIENT and
VIOLET AND THE HIDDEN
TREASURE

AND DON'T MISS
VIOLET'S NEXT
ADVENTURE,
COMING SPRING 2017.